POEMS, PROSE & ....
A light-hearted look at life and
language through the eyes of a
Yorkshire Lass

From one of Sheffield's Bestselling
Authors

Jacqueline Creek

Enjoy reading the Book

Jacquelin Creek

i

First Published in 2018 by Jacqueline Creek
Written by Jacqueline Creek
Editing by Anne Grange Editing
Text and Photographs Copyright © Jacqueline
Creek 2018

ISBN
9781718117518

A little book of things you always wanted to know that you didn't want to know!

Contents

Dip into the contents in any order. Keep this book handy...next to your favourite armchair, on your bedside table, or even to while away the time in the smallest room in the house; it will entertain you for years...but which is poetry, which is prose, and which is tripe? There's only one way to find out!

THE GENERAL'S WAR

It was a cold Sunday morning, the air quite still,
As the soldiers assembled at the foot of the hill,
They shuffled, and breathed warm air to their hands,
All ready to follow their leader's commands.

One man stood before them, taller than most,
Steel eyes unblinking, back straight as a post,
His medals outshone the gleam of his boots,
A General – Proud, in his uniform suit.

They waited in earnest – for his voice in their ears,
But the man stood unmoving, calm, without fear.
Head back and chin thrust out like a fist,
Surveying his followers, not one would he miss.

He suddenly blinked himself out of his thoughts,
Breathing now shallow, jaw clenched and taut,
Bracing forward he cried out to his men –
'The order is given – we march at ten'.

Silence now broken, they mustered as one,
Husbands, fathers, brothers and sons.
He glanced at his watch, one minute to go –
Then forward with purpose, not one would say no.

A baton was tossed high into the air,
The General commenced with his favourite prayer,
His foot was first forward as they slipped into line,
Shoulder to shoulder they stepped out in time.

He swung forth his arms, ahead of his men,
The battle hymn blared as the church clock struck ten –
'*Onward Christian Soldiers...*' they stomped to the beat,
And the Salvation Army band marched down the street.

Shortlisted in Writing Magazine
Open Rhymed Poetry Competition
April 2016

FOR PETE'S SAKE

Can anyone tell me who Pete is, please?

I'm sure some of you would like to know too. I'm fed up of doing or not doing things for Pete. While we're talking about Pete, why is Larry so happy? Also, who is Jack Robinson? Why do we say, 'before I could say Jack Robinson'? Who the dickens is he?

How come we don't say, 'Before I could say Alan McIntosh,' or 'Albert Watson,' and why would I want to say his name if I don't know him, and Gordon Bennett for that matter, and why say, 'for that matter', if it doesn't matter, then why say it? Argy!

Who can prove Bill Stickers is innocent? Perhaps Murphy, lawman, can answer that one. Why did Fanny Adams feel the need to be sweet? What other reason would anyone have to go to the foot of their stairs unless they were going to bed? And why do some people think we'd be daft enough to take the kitchen sink on holiday?

That's another one, 'kick the bucket'. If someone's on their death bed, why would they want to get up and kick a bucket before they depart?'

Does anyone know of a fate worse than death? Has anyone come back and said, 'Well, that wasn't as bad as I thought. It was much worse when I fell down the stairs and broke both legs.'

And does it matter if a rolling stone gathers no moss, who cares? And for Pete's sake, who the devil would keep a skeleton in their cupboard, or ride a high horse knowing how difficult it would be to get off?

'Many a little makes a mickle; many a mickle makes a muckle.' It makes me wonder what some of these writers were on.

What about this guy with a hunch-back and hooked nose, Punch? He had nothing to be so pleased about, beating his wife, Judy and the baby, along with his dog Toby, for stealing the sausages; then bragging, 'That's the way to do it.'

Something I always did want to know was what the Hokey Cokey song and dance was all about. So after putting my whole self in and my whole self out a few times, I found out that really is what it's all about.

Whoever thought this one up hasn't lived. 'A woman needs a man like a fish needs a bicycle? 'Could a fish actually defrost the car on a winter's morning?

If you're married to a doctor, does it mean you can't eat apples? I suppose that depends on how long you've been married!

While we're on the subject of idioms and sayings, here are a few of my favourites.

- ☞ Never be afraid to try something new. Remember, amateurs built the ark. Professionals built the Titanic.

- ☞ Be careful the light at the end of the tunnel isn't an oncoming train.

- ☞ Practice safe eating, always use condiments.

- ☞ If you suffer from kleptomania, take something for it.

- ☞ I'm not a perfectionist. My parents were though.

- ☞ Don't read their rubbish, read mine.

- ☞ Better to remain silent and be thought a fool than to speak and remove all doubt.

- ☞ If you think your boss is stupid, remember: you wouldn't have a job if he was smarter.

- ☞ You're so stupid, if you threw a rock at the ground, you'd miss.

- ☞ Be yourself – No one else wants to be you.

- ☞ Boys will be boys. (Try getting away with that today)

- ☞ One day you're the Cock of the North – Next day, a feather duster.

5

AN EYE FOR DETAIL

I was in junior school when I first noted that art and craft were my best subjects. I won a set of Reeves watercolour paints after entering a junior painting competition for Ringtons Tea. Colourful trays set in a shiny black tin, which I was too afraid to use for fear of spoiling them.

Art always remained my best subject. I made posters and eye-catching window displays at the chemist's shop where I worked after leaving school at fifteen. As I moved on, my creativity, no longer required in other employment, was only used while decorating and designing my room layouts to capture the best details.

Years later, when I established my own business, for the strangest of reasons, I faced the biggest challenge of all, which awakened my dormant creativity into another field, designing costumes. From Vicars and Nuns to Regal and formal, stone age to space age. Kings and Queens, from all eras; I'll tell you something more about this later.

Cartoon characters and film stars, pop stars, superstars. Oceanic creatures – octopus, prawns, lobsters and dolphins, birds from up high, to the tamest and wildest of animals. A forty-foot dragon for the Up

Helly Aa Festival in Lerwick, a Pudsey Bear for the BBC. A Billy the Blood-drop costume for the Kidney Foundation. Elephants, dinosaurs, hamsters and mice. Pantomime characters, Popes, Archbishops, French maids and French tarts, Army, Naval and Air force uniforms, 20s, 30s, 40s, 50s, 60s, 70s and 80s – costumes from each era...

We sent Vikings to Norway; Polar bears to Iceland, Kangaroos to Oz, Grass skirts to Hawaii and Belly Dancers to Dubai. Oh-oh! I feel a poem coming on. I'll see if I can finish it before the end of the book.

The 40-foot Chinese dragon we made for "Up Helly Aa" Shetland Isles. We didn't have enough people to fill the full length!

PAIN AND CREATIVITY

Northern General Hospital, Sheffield. 17th
September 1997

I opened my eyes and cried as the pain shot through me.

'Jacqueline, Jacqueline, it's all right.'

A friendly face smiled down at me. A gentle hand squeezed my shoulder. The bed I was lying in began to move. I closed my eyes. The next time I woke, I was more aware of the pain and my surroundings. I was in a side ward at the Northern General Hospital.

'You're awake.' The friendly face I had seen earlier appeared again. I tried to sit up, and the pain struck deep in my tummy.

'Don't try to sit up, Jacqueline. I'll raise the bed.' A moment later, the back of the bed was raised. 'I'm Julie, your nurse; press this button if you need me.' She placed the call controller on the bed. 'And this one regulates the morphine for your pain.'

I hoped it had a LARGE bottle attached to the other end, and pressed the button repeatedly.

'Don't worry, you can't overdose,' she said. 'The anaesthetist will be along to see you shortly.'

It was the day of my fifty-third birthday, and I was coming round from a Hysterectomy, an operation for cervical cancer. To give it its proper title, it was a Bilateral Salpingo-Oophorectomy – in other words, everything within snatching distance of the surgeon's knife. I remembered the toilet roll Happy Birthday banner the nursing staff had made and strung across the doorway when I was taken to the theatre that morning, and how they all sang Happy Birthday as the Gas Man sent me into the land of make-believe.

My stay in hospital was to be a long one, ten days. Ten long days, but with a bit of luck, I could be out by the weekend. Considering it was only Wednesday, it was a long shot.

I fidgeted a little and tested my pain threshold. Hmm! not good. I pressed the button. My head felt clammy, and I felt sick. As I lay there, I wondered when we first recognise pain. I could remember falling many times as a child and running home to Mum to bathe grazed knees and cover with Germolene and a strip of old pillow-case for a bandage, followed by a kiss to make it better.

Did we feel pain at an earlier age? When my brother and sister were teething, they cried all the time. I fell asleep knowing we feel pain from the moment we are born: that's why we cry as we take our first breath.

I read somewhere that if you are in severe pain; it helps if you write about it. One of the nurses saw me deep in thought as she inserted a pain-killer suppository where the sun doesn't shine.

'Why don't you paint your pain away, Jacqueline, you said art was once your thing?'

How can you paint away pain? I thought as the pain-killing drug melted into the confines of my bowels. Then I had an idea.

The following evening, John arrived with pens, pencils, charcoals and crayons. When he and all the visitors had left, and the lights were turned down low, I took a sheet of white cartridge paper and with red and black pens and crayons, began my artistic creation: ***Pain!***

'What's that supposed to be?' said one of the nurses next morning.

'What the devil's that?' said John when he came to visit.

'PAIN! It's my interpretation of pain. It's abstract – think of Jackson Pollock, Damien Hirst. It's expressionism.'

'I can't see any animals in formaldehyde.'

'No! I can't either...It's how he portrays death. I'm portraying pain.'

'Are you sure they haven't operated on your brain, Jack?'

I slowly recovered from the hysterical-ectomy, as I now called it. It was Saturday afternoon, three days after the op and most of the staff were on their breaks. Lying in bed, watching *Carry on Doctor* on a small TV in my sideward, I was in hysterics and agony. There was no remote controller to turn the TV or sound off, I couldn't get out of bed unaided, and I couldn't summon a nurse. The more I laughed, the more my stitches pulled.

As I had to take it easy after leaving the hospital, I continued with my drawing, sketching in charcoal and colouring in pastel. I was eventually allowed to go abroad, for some much-needed sunshine − 'only small amounts' − the consultant's words. My desire to sketch and paint vanished and I found my thoughts carried to more melodious forms of artistic creations, so in the warmth of Tenerife, I began dabbling in writing poetry. Some people, after hearing examples would say, How not to write poetry.

This is the first one I wrote...

TO PARADISE

Who has not
Flown the nest of England on an icy winter day,
In a capsule, rise on wings of steel
Up through dark clouds to see below,
Strange lands amidst the blue.

To wake next morn
Where tall palms sway, and almonds scent the air,
Sweet blossoms bloom, and olives ripe,
Burst forth and spill their fruit.

Who has not
Trod the water's edge, sand shifting under feet,
Collected shells – such childish joys,
And listened to the sea.

Where
Whales and dolphins bask in the surf, and with such
Awesome power – rise, then plunge –
Oceanic depths, performing for the watcher.

Who has not
Seen where cockatiels and parakeets fly freely overhead,
And higher still on currents warm, large gulls
Float on the breeze, effortlessly drifting, defying gravity.

And give
One's body to the sun, it slowly to uncurl,
Drinking of its power – flesh and blood's reborn,
As warmth and light unlocks set bones, and grey begins
To fade, and all that mattered yesterday
Is now very far away.

To see
The days melt into evening, and hear cicadas call,
And the fiery heavenly furnace, sink slowly into the sea,
Bathing the world in crimson dusted with old gold,
Then close your eyes in wonder and promise to return.

First published in 'Pick Me Up'
Anchor Books 1997

FINDING BARNEY

It wasn't long before I began writing about my pets, in Winter Fishing, in which I give Barney a 'walk-on' part. But in Barney's case, it was more of a 'run-on and off' part.

Let me tell you about Barney. Barney was an Old English sheepdog. He looked like one, white and grey, thick fluffy coat, floppy ears, and ambling gait, but that's where the similarity ends. He wasn't our first Old English, but he was our first seriously-mental-problem dog, and he was huge. Standing twenty-seven inches at the shoulder, he was as tall as me when he jumped up. We collected him from the rescue centre in Welshpool, which is a long way from Penistone – which took even longer on a foggy day in late November.

At two years old, he had lived in eight different homes and several kennels in the hope of finding him a permanent home. All to no avail. No one could cope with him.

I no longer had my beautiful, gentle Muffin and knew I could never replace him, but we did have room for another dog, and my other two were both bitches. Living near to where we worked meant we could easily walk the dogs there and back, and they could remain with us throughout the day, each dog having its favourite place in the office, sewing room or shop and of course, the canteen.

However, this lovely peaceful routine was now coming to an end.

We were late arriving at our destination in Welshpool, owing to the weather and getting stuck in a snow-covered ditch where we had to wait for a farmer with a tractor to come along and tow us out for £20. There were no mobile phones in those days and no phone boxes on country lanes in Wales.

After meeting with the manager of the rescue centre and handing over £50 for Barney, we had to follow her car to a farm, a further twenty-five miles into the Welsh countryside to collect him. As soon as we arrived, she spoke a few words in Welsh to the farmer, then turned and left.

We got out of the car and followed the man into the farmhouse. The man was having a conversation with himself as he was speaking in Welsh. John and I looked at each other and grinned. From what I could make out, he had to fetch the dog from somewhere further afield, and it would take another forty minutes for him to collect the dog and return.

We sat waiting. The farmhouse was old and needed serious repairs. The wife – I presume it was his wife – sat in a rocking chair near a coal fire, knitting. The only sounds were the ticking of the clock on the mantelpiece and the sheep's heads, bubbling away in a pot on top of the Aga, the flickering flames in the fire grate. She slowly got up and drew the curtains. The squeak of the rocker added to the medley of sounds.

'Fog's getting bad,' she said in a combination of Welsh and English, and went back to the fireplace and gave the coals a poke.

My stomach lurched, it was getting dark, and we had a long, long way to go home. I consoled myself with thoughts of the young dog desperately in need of a home and wondered if he would resemble Muffin in any way. I smiled to myself and thrilled at the prospect of having a new dog in the house. I had been a long time getting over Muffin.

A loud scuffling noise suddenly came from the doorway as the door banged open. The farmer, red face and winded, entered, grabbing the side of the door to keep himself upright while holding on to the odd eyed, deafeningly loud barking beast he had on a chain.

I'll tell you more about Barney later. Meanwhile, here's the poem I wrote after an incident while out walking with Barney.

The one and only Barney

WINTER FISHING

I woke at dawn and drank a hasty cup of tea,
A good day for fishing I was sure it would be.
I packed some snap, my rod and some bait,
Wellies and keep-net – to get a good spot I couldn't be
late.
With thoughts of Barbels, Chubbs and Bream
Put my tackle in the car and drove off down the street.

The river looked cold in the pale winter sun
Which made me shudder, and my feet turn numb.
I baited my hook and cast into the deep –
A fifteen-pound Barbel I was sure I would reap.
The hours rolled by as I dozed on the edge
But my float was still upright, so I threw in some bread –

Maggots and castor, but the fish still wouldn't bite,
Conditions were perfect with no one in sight.
No sooner said, than a woman appeared
Calling her dog which fell on deaf ears,
As he raced towards me with a great bounding gait
And clumsily plonked his front paws in my bait.

While I watched all my maggots wriggle into the ground
His slobbering chops my packed lunched he'd found.
'Barney – Come here boy!' But in vain she did call
As he gobbled up my pork pie, wrapper and all.
'I'm ever so sorry – he's still young and daft.'
She called, pursuing Barney who'd got away fast.

Mayhem spurned, I re-baited the line
With my one remaining maggot, and looked at the time,
The morning now gone, I shivered with cold
As the rod in my fingers, I barely could hold.

I placed it beside me and opened my flask. Mmmm, steaming hot soup.
What more could I ask...? A pork pie! I smiled, warmed through with the broth.

Stomach now filled and spirits renewed
I settled back down for a good afternoon.
I dozed – still watching the bob of my float,
Suddenly sneezed, coughed, and felt a pain in my throat.
At half past three, the light began fading
No Roach, Chubb or Barbel, nor even a Grayling.

I reeled in my line; all it took was one look
At the one remaining maggot still skewered on the hook.
So I called it a day and packed up my things,
Yawned, and stretched out my cold aching limbs.
And stamping my feet, blew warm air to my hands,
My thoughts now of home and a steaming hot bath.

So, grasping my tackle and clutching dead grass clumps
I hauled myself up from the slippery mud bank...
Right into the path of a solitary walker –
Head bowed and tucked in averting the weather.
'Sorry,' I mumbled as drops rolled down my nose.
'Caught owt?' he answered.
'Naa, just a flippin' cold.'

BARNEY COMES HOME

'What have we done?'

Bumper to bumper along all three lanes of the M6 and we still had to cross the Pennines with Barney, who had been kept in a barn or probably the pigsty if his smell was anything to go by, and looked more like a bedraggled, unsheared sheep than an Old English Sheepdog.

Despite six sleeping tablets, he barked and jumped all over the car on the way home. Dog cage? Never needed one before and where would we acquire one at this time of the morning – and a muzzle?

It was 3am when we finally arrived home, and it didn't stop there. Amy and Emma, my two bitches, knew instinctively that another dog was in the house and came running down the stairs. They barked and growled and Barney barked back. My head was thumping; all I wanted was to sleep.

Great game, thought Barney, jumping all over them. I took the two girls upstairs to bed, but they wouldn't settle. They could hear the big guy downstairs and insisted on letting him know who was boss. John was angry, he was tired, filthy, stunk of every farmyard beast, and so did I. I wondered if we would ever rid ourselves, the car, and the house, of the smell.

Weeks later, after falling down the stairs a few times while trying to attack the Grandfather clock standing in the hallway, and finally knocking it over on top of him, Barney realised the clock was not going to stop chiming. The two girls gradually got used to him, but were always ready with a quick snap if he overstepped the mark.

Barney was the proverbial Gentle Giant, yet his bark could make cups rattle in their saucers. He had no road sense; in fact, I don't think he had any sense. He couldn't be let off the lead as he thought cars were toys to play with. Sheep and cows in surrounding fields were for chasing, and visitors, however tall, were given full-facial licks.

The doorbell rang one afternoon. Barney barked and rushed down the hallway towards the frosted glass door, slamming into it as he came to a halt, Emma and Amy followed. The chap standing on the other side jumped back. I struggled to open the door slightly, just enough to see what he wanted.

'Sorry,' he said and looked at my hands and legs trying to hold back three barking dogs as he cautiously uplifted his tool kit and began to retreat. 'I've come to fit the burglar alarm and obviously got the wrong house.'

Outside our house we had a small lawn, a few shrubs and plants, and a five-foot-high wall, where our neighbour's cat often sat cleaning himself. It didn't bother Emma and Amy; as long as it didn't venture into the house, peace existed. Barney thought differently: he saw the cat had four legs, and that meant only one thing –Chase!

A couple of days after the burglar alarm fitter incident, our neighbour knocked on our door.

'Can you come and get your Barney? – he's got his head stuck in the cat flap.'

One Sunday morning, we set off to Skegness. Amy and Emma lay on their beds at the back of the seats in the van, excited at the thought of going somewhere different. Barney, despite also having a bed, preferred to stand at the back and look out of the back window, barking at everything in the distance. Anyone overtaking would do so at our risk. Barney would race from the back of the van to the front and try to clamber on to the front seats, trampling Emma and Amy in the process, who would then retaliate. A slap of my hand on the dashboard usually ended the conflict.

We stopped in Willingham Woods for a mid-way break and pulled into the car park. Looking around to see if any other dogs were around, John slowly opened the side-door on the van with lead in hand, ready to grab Barney. But Barney was too quick and dived straight out, running over to the car opposite where a man was helping an elderly woman onto the back seat of the car. Barney saw an open door, pushed past the people and jumped up and onto the back seat.

'Oh my God, what's happening?' The woman fell backwards as the man managed to catch her and looked around to see who the irresponsible dog owners were.

'Is this your bloody dog?' he shouted to someone who was just exiting their car. The man looked back at him as if he'd had too much sun.

Meanwhile, we had made a hasty unseen retreat into the woods. 'Quick, keep walking,' I said to John, while not letting Emma or Amy stop for a sniff. A minute later, Barney came bounding and panting along the path and straight into the back of my legs.

Barney never changed, and we never gave up, even though every visit to the vet meant entry and exit by the back door, and despite well-meaning friends telling us to have him put down. Never, Barney had had too many homes in the past.

The first time we saw him, we knew that he would always be a handful, despite being castrated to quieten him down, which he had to have as he only had one testicle. For all his exuberance, he lived eleven more years. Rest in Peace Barney Boy—with all your faults, you were loved.

We vowed never to take on a problem dog again after Barney; we were getting too old, but time heals, and within a year we had acquired another, even worse than Barney, but a fraction of his size. A Cross-Patterdale Terrier, aka The Terror. I can't tell you about Pippa as she's going to write her own story. She says I will only 'humanise' it.

THE LAMPLIGHTER

Arising first while others slumber,
Flat cap askew,
Silently at dawn and dusk,
He treads the streets
From lamp to lamp,
His cheery whistle little more than a whisper.

Spirit-filled lamp in hand
His ladder hooked upon cross bars
Two small chains to stop or start the flow of gas
To shed pale light and flood the gloom or dim the lamp.
The pane of glass swings open
Skilled fingers ply.

Mantles crumble with one's touch
Watchman of the night.
Local sinecure.
Now long gone,
His ghost still walks the empty streets.
When daylight dawns, his footsteps and
A whistle carries on the wind.

INTERLUDE

Ooh! I'm getting all maudlin now. Let's have a bit of humour. Before we do, here's a little sporting question for you. Which world-famous fighter was knocked down in every fight, yet still got up and won?

I'm now going to leave you and make a cuppa. Meanwhile, here are a few bits of information you might want to know...and some you might not!

Stone spiral staircases in medieval castles ran clockwise. Because all the knights were right-handed, and when the invading armies came running up the steps, they would not be able to use their right hands which were holding their swords because of the difficulties caused while climbing the curvature of the steps. Left-handed knights would have no trouble, except that left-handed people couldn't become knights as they were supposedly descendants of the devil.

Warning: don't read the following fact while eating.

Did you know there is a bus that travels between Bath and Bristol, and is powered by human poo? This environmentally-friendly, 40-seater, runs on gas generated from the treatment of sewage. One bus-load of passengers can provide enough power for it to travel the length of Britain and back; a distance of 1,760 miles.

What I'd like to know is, have the seats been replaced with toilets?

TIME TRAVEL

People in the Spanish border town of Sanlúcar de Guadiana can cross into neighbouring Portugal by zip wire – and travel backwards in time. I kid you not. Passengers cross the Guadiana River, which separates Spain from the Portuguese town of Alcoutim, travelling at 45 miles per hour down the half-mile gradient.

Although the journey lasts barely a minute, it crosses a time zone, so they arrive in Portugal about an hour before they left!

HUH?

A researcher walked past a radar tube and a chocolate bar in his pocket melted. He then went on to invent the microwave.

A QUICK CLUE

Have you discovered the answer to the sporting question yet? No, I'll give you a clue. He was American.

THE SEVEN DWARFS

Before deciding on the names for the seven dwarfs we know today, Disney considered: Chesty, Tubby, Burpy, Deafy, Hickey, Wheezy, and Awful.

DID YOU KNOW?

Charlie Chaplin once won third prize in a Charlie Chaplin look-alike contest.

HMM...!

The male giraffe determines a female's fertility by tasting her urine. If it passes the test, the courtship continues...Each to their own, I suppose.

BOOM

Peanuts are one of the ingredients of dynamite.

BOOM BOOM

In ten minutes, a hurricane releases more energy than all the nuclear weapons combined.

DARE TO BE DIFFERENT –
5 THINGS TO DO IN A LIFT

- Pull an agonizing face while smacking your forehead and muttering: 'Shut up, all of you just shut UP!'
- Open your bag/briefcase and ask: 'Got enough air in there?'
- Meow occasionally.

- Say 'Ding!' at each level.
- When arriving at your floor, grunt and strain to yank the doors open, and then act embarrassed when they open by themselves.

TALKING OF LIFTS...

Have you heard of a Paternoster lift? It's a strange contraption. For one thing, it doesn't have doors; its open cabins run slowly in a continuous loop and it doesn't stop to allow passengers on or off at their destination floor. I suppose you could call it a Hop on-Hop off lift.

There are very few left nowadays. Safety concerns began to emerge after a series of accidents, and in 1970, construction ceased. Only a few remain, one is installed in The Arts Tower – part of Sheffield University and the tallest academic building in the UK, and is also the tallest operational lift of its kind in Europe. The Paternoster was built in 1960 with 38 2-person carriages, along with two standard lifts; it serves the 78-metre tall building.

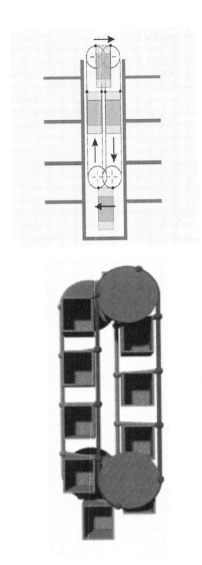

This is how the Paternoster lift keeps moving!

THE VISITOR

He came and stopped by my feet
I was sitting by the pond,
Fish hiding beneath the lilies
The yellow Koi saw me, plopped
And plunged into the depths.

I looked at the stranger by my side
And took a deep breath: he was dark,
Menacing. I looked away
And then back. He was alone

And I – ready to run. I glanced around.
High in the trees, the Doves cooed.
The waterfall trickled,
Slow, with the summer drought.

He moved nearer. His face covered unseen.
A chill caressed my spine.
I closed my eyes and breathed
Deep, then deeper.

My mantra. Be stilled. Peace.
He will not harm me. He cannot harm me.
My eyes opened.
He crawled away...

Did you guess the answer to the sporting question? Here, I'll tell you: it was Popeye. I didn't say he was a boxer, did I?

***

HOW I GOT INTO WRITING

When I retired and began writing, I realised that I lacked writing skills, especially as the last thirty-odd years had been taken up with writing nothing other than business letters and demands for payments. And for most of that time, my secretary did the letter writing. Letters of friendship were gradually replaced with phone calls, followed by emails and texting.

Knowing I would be last in line for a Wordsmith badge, I had to do something, but what? At almost seventy years old, I was limited, but I had an insatiable quest for knowledge, if only to prove that you can teach an old dog new tricks, even though I can't remember where I've buried my bone.

So I joined a writing group and thereby discovered a 'last chance' college. Their mission:

'To provide outstanding adult residential and community education for the empowerment and transformation of individuals and communities.'

The Northern College is in one of the most beautiful and impressive settings in the north of England. It is located at Wentworth Castle, Stainborough, just three and a half miles from Barnsley town centre.

Wentworth Castle was the home of the Earls of Strafford during the 18th century, when most of the existing buildings on the site were built, along with the surrounding park and gardens. The main house is a Grade 1 listed building of outstanding historical importance and is surrounded by the only Grade 1 listed landscape in South Yorkshire.

Its thirty-eight acres of grounds and gardens are of outstanding botanical and environmental interest. The gardens contain many varieties of rhododendron, camellia, magnolia and other Asiatic flowering plants, as well as native European species, and in May and June each year, their dazzling blooms attract many visitors. Together with the surrounding park and woodland, they make up a welcoming habitat for birds, insects, small mammals, fungi and wildflowers.

Wentworth Castle has been used for educational purposes since it was sold to the Barnsley local authority in the late 1940s, and modern teaching and residential accommodation blocks have been added to the site. A new phase of conversion and building is now beginning to improve existing facilities, and provide for planned future expansion.

The Metropolitan Borough of Barnsley consists of the town of Barnsley itself, and a number of surrounding towns and villages, whose total population is 230,000. The area has a long history, and its traditional industries have been coal-mining, agriculture, glass manufacture, iron and steel work and engineering.

Coal-mining was the dominant industry until the 1980s. In 1984, British Coal provided 20,000 jobs in Barnsley. The closure of the deep mines in the area since then has transformed many aspects of life. Barnsley, like its near neighbours Sheffield, Rotherham and Doncaster, is a town undergoing large-scale economic and cultural change.

The college is dedicated to the education and training of men and women who are without formal qualifications.

Having never been to college, I wasn't bothered about certificates, having proved my worth by becoming self-employed and starting my own business. Employing over thirty people, manufacturing, retailing and exporting, was good enough for me. But what about the people out there who wanted to read my life story and my whacky poems? These books would have to consist of more than a Dear Sir and Yours Faithfully.

So, as I listened to the induction and chose some English-related courses, I became aware of how much the educational system had changed since I was at school, and realised I had bought houses with less formality.

Unperturbed by knowing I would be the oldest pupil in the classes, I was there to learn and learn I would. And learn I did. When I left, I was confident with my new knowledge of creative writing, and knew enough about left-wing politics to pen a book. But not likely to!

In all seriousness, Northern College and the tutors do a great job, and it is an excellent place for people who are unqualified or need retraining and looking for work or better positions. Keep up the good work, Northern College.

Northern College – a grand place for learning!

37

POETRY FOR BEGINNERS

What do you think of the poetry, so far? According to Marshall Gass, good poetry comes from understanding the devices that make it work. It grabs the imagination and adds a dimension which the mind understands but is not so easy to translate into prose paragraphs and sentences!

Any wiser? No, neither am I. I have been a member of a poetry group for three years and am no more advanced than when I joined. The other members write some perfect poetry, which you will read later. But I just cannot get my head around alliterations, anapaests, assonances, caesuras, cantos, consonances, couplets, enjambment, idioms, haikus, hyperboles, onomatopoeias, and stanzas, which are all poetic terms. And to be honest, I don't want to. At the age of 73, life's too short.

I've created my own version of these poetic terms and their meanings, which is good enough for me, and I hope, for you. If anything I write falls into the above categories, then it's purely by accident or luck, whichever way you want to interpret it.

POETIC TERMS

Alliteration To make minor adjustments

Anapest Frenzied movements following a snake bite

Assonance A non-religious forgiveness ceremony

Caesura Old Roman monetary unit

Canto A Chinese pantomime

Consonance Having great patience

Couplet A state of being born with two left feet

Enjambment A pyjama party

Idiom A group of politicians

Haiku A sneeze occurring while giving thanks

Hyperbole Downhill bowling alley

Juxtaposition? There's a name to conjure with

Onomatopoeia Mountain Range bordering Tibet and China

Stanza Brazilian dance similar to Rumba

Any proper poets reading this will by now have put the book into the bin. Those reading on Kindle will be tearing their hair out, searching for the delete button. Ahh! Not so easy on a Kindle. To delete anything on mine, I have to hook up to a laptop. It's one of the earlier designs, the first one after we stopped using a slate board and chalk.

FAVOURITE POEMS

I did enjoy poetry at school, but not all of it. Shakespeare, Emily Dickinson and Keats, I found so boring.

What I did enjoy, and can't forget is the mind-set created and feeling of being mentally charged as I read Tennyson's 'Charge of the Light Brigade.'

Half a league, half a league,
Half a league onward,
All in the valley of Death
Rode the six hundred.

Can't you just feel the mounting tension and hear the horses' hooves, their cries of fear as they ride towards the enemy?

And Alfred Noyes, who wrote, 'The Highwayman.'

And the highwayman came riding –
Riding – riding –
The highwayman came riding, up to the old inn-door.

You can feel the galloping pace of the highwayman; hear the clattering hooves on the cobbles and the rat-a-tat-tat on the shutters.

Who remembers 'Cargoes' by John Masefield?

Quinquireme of Nineveh from distant Ophir,
Rowing home to haven in sunny Palestine.

There would have been 150 galley-slaves toiling away in the bowels of the ship. Six men to each forty-five-foot-long oar. Whooosh, whoosh, whoosh.

How about the:

Stately Spanish galleon coming from the Isthmus,
Dipping through the tropics...

The sea-breeze, slowly deflating her sails as she neared port.

Then the:

Dirty British Coaster with its salt-baked smoke-stack
Butting through the channel...

The chug-chug of the engines as she pushed through home waters.

These poems, like songs, have rhythm. These well-loved poems all have one thing in common – they take you there, you experience it.

In 1960, Johnny Tillotson released a record called 'Poetry in Motion.' It was nothing to do with poems; it was a love song. But I think it describes verse such as the above.

41

Well, the poems in this book are nothing like those classic masterpieces. In my book, you'll find humour, satire, empathy, in fact, a bit of everything.

Do you remember Robert Frost's poem, 'The Road not Taken?'

Here's my version: 'I took the road not taken – and now I'm lost...'

POSSESSION

You lie beside me on my bed
Your agile body lean and dark,
So masculine in movement
Handsome in its form.

Neck stretched and bared submissively
Inhibitions you have none,
As you press your body closer –
You are my chosen one.

Your dark brown eyes show only love
As they gaze into my own
Unblinking adoration –
Darkening with desire.

Driven by your basic needs
You climb atop my outstretched limbs
And hold me firmly with your weight,
While heavy breathing fills the air

Your urgent kisses fill my ears –
My nose, my lips, my mouth
Oh, stop it, Blackie, that's enough
You're the most possessive dog I've known.

First published in 'All Creatures Great and Small'
Triumph House, 2000

Ah! That got you, you were wondering where this was going weren't you? Be honest.

43

MEMORIES OF BLACKPOOL

I wrote this poem for a group of fun loving fifty-plus-year-olds who spent a weekend in Blackpool during October 1991

Golden October with its autumn chill
Sent us to Blackpool, our hearts and minds to fill
With merriment, laughter and happiness to share
With friends and loved ones the joys awaiting there.
Memories of pier shows and musicals, unwelcoming
Bars, tram rides, taxis and illuminated cars.

The days and night so full of laughter,
How we ached the morning after. The dressing up and
Dressing down and the mile long walks back from the
town.
Memories of waxworks, Sea-world, sweet tasting wine,
Chip shops, sex shops, puppies caged in pet-shops.

The silly rides that were such fun, we thought alike,
We were as one. Our age no barrier to childish joys –
Suggestive hats, slot machines, and soft furry toys.
Memories of ghost trains, giant slides, helter-skelters,
Moving stairs, roundabouts and fast spinning chairs.

The time to leave came far too soon, our happy hearts
Now filled with gloom. But leave we must, we'd had
Our hour, and no time left to climb the tower.
Memories of swimming pools, Jacuzzis, buskers,
Bright-coloured vans, photographs, and mist-covered
sand.

We packed our bags and hugged and kissed, the last few
Days would be sadly missed. For now, we had to face the
Truth – and leave behind our regained youth.
Memories of Blackpool, Golden October with its
Autumn chill.

We'll have some more poems later, but now I want to tell you about flash fiction.

WHAT IS FLASH FICTION?

It is a style of fictional literature of extreme brevity and, like any other fictional work, should have a beginning, middle and an end, although not particularly in that order.

You will find writers each have their definition of how it should be done. For example one particular writer, I'll not mention his name, but it's David Gaffney; he states that it should start in the middle. Why? I ask myself. He even states the ending shouldn't be at the end!

Where should it be then?

Flash Fiction (or FF for short) for me is a short story, extra short, short-short in fact and sometimes called micro-fiction. It can consist of as few as six words; I'll give you an example of this in a minute. There can be six words or a thousand, with variations in between. It shouldn't be too laborious or tedious to read: there are plenty of lengthier stories out there for that. When I'm writing FF, which is usually while I am having a break from my lengthier work, I use the KISS principle. (Keep It Simple, Stupid.)

Get to the point. People who are reading FF are usually in a hurry, on overcrowded public transport, eyes glued to iPhone's/iPads. No time to read a lengthy story, no room to open a newspaper or magazine. Continuous interruptions – *Excuse me, can I get past? The bus/train/tram/taxi will be here any minute. Class starts in a minute.*

The attention span is short-lived. Keep it short and easy to read. Here is the six word story I mentioned:-

It is often attributed to Ernest Hemingway. The link to him is unsubstantiated as similar stories predate him. This is how it goes: Hemingway, while dining with friends, supposedly bets them that he can write an entire story in six words. Bets are placed and Hemingway writes on a napkin:

FOR SALE - BABY SHOES - NEVER WORN.

He passes it around the table and collects his winnings. But it was said that the original version was previously published in a newspaper and was actually a baby carriage instead of shoes. The narrator contacted the seller to offer his condolences, only to learn that the sale was due to the birth of twins rather than a single child!

We're going to start with a few very short ones.

THE HOUSE AT THE TOP OF THE AVENUE

I paused for a moment before entering the tree-lined avenue and saw the big house at the top. My legs weakened as I continued walking. The front door and curtains were closed. Towards the back, a path led into a flower-filled garden. Walking around it, I smelled the different scents and then came to a shed, the door slightly open. I peered inside; there was nothing of interest to me. Then I saw a pile of sacks on the floor and laid myself down. Perfect, just what an old stray dog needs.

THE STRUGGLE

I saw the fear in his eyes and wanted to help. I held my breath as he struggled to his feet and his arms reached out. I knelt, willing his legs to have strength, and then my fears turned to joy. My baby took his first faltering steps towards me.

BLOWING AWAY THE COBWEBS

'Come on, Bob, let's blow the cobwebs away.' We walked to the cricket ground, sat on a bench and looked up to the sky.

'This is just what we need, peace, after all those noisy relatives filling the house over Christmas. Listen, Bob, silence.'

I pulled my Beanie hat over my ears and looked across at the naked trees.

Bob sat, stared, and then yawned. His breath rose from his mouth into the frosty air. I patted his shoulder. 'Come on, let's walk a bit further.' He jumped off the bench; his paws disappearing into the soft snow.

A WALK IN THE PARK

Sandra walked into the park and sat on her favourite bench. Autumn leaves rustled around her feet. She looked up at the near-naked trees foretelling the coming of winter. People hurried by, heads low against the breeze.

Sandra remembered happier times, when Colin and she had walked through this park to the bowling alley. Perhaps she might see him today. A man came and sat on the bench. She smiled, but he took out his phone and began texting. After five minutes, he left.

I'll wait a few minutes longer, she thought. A woman walked towards her, smiling. She sat by Sandra.

'Are you all right, love?' she asked.

Sandra stared at her. 'You can see me?'

MUM'S TREASURE CHEST

I sat with my elbows on the table; fists cupped beneath my chin and stared out of the rain-lashed window. My cricket bat stood by the door. I sighed. Mum put down the iron and took a faded tin box from the cupboard and placed it on the table.

'Here, sort them out if you want something to do.'

I looked at the scratched image of a thatched cottage, eased off the lid and stared at the contents: pirates' booty. Jewels from distant lands, reflected in my eyes as I lifted handfuls of emeralds and rubies, opals, and pearls, sapphires and aquamarines.

I could smell the sea air and feel the salt water spray on my face as the marauding pirates brandished cutlasses and pistols, swinging from Galleon to Galleon on Caribbean seas, sails and shirtsleeves flapping. Chests full of treasures hoisted and hauled from ship to ship. Screams and cries as the dead and dying sank into the sea. Smoking canons spent and fallen, bows rising and falling with the swell, broken masthead, crash, boom.

I picked up another handful and sorted them into sections. What's that doing in here? I stared at the round dull brown object. 'I'm glad you've found that, 'said Mum. Your father's got a button missing on his overcoat.

PAYBACK

It was a hot sticky night when I went to bed. A long day and long-fought battle meant I could now rest and reflect on my conquest. Sleep would come easy. I crawled into bed and switched out the light.

Then they appeared. Three came through the doorway, metallic figures glistening in the moonlight. Their ten-foot frames lowered as they entered. Another trio behind them and then another.

I threw the sheet off the bed and dashed to the balcony door. The cooler night air rushed in. Three more stood on the balcony, no, six, nine. Weapons primed, held close to their chests. Aliens. Payback time. I had killed their first and second platoon, not en-masse, but with stealth, three by three.

There was nowhere to hide. I looked over the balcony rail. More were down below, groups of three moving as one in the semi-darkness.

My spine chilled. I no longer had my weapon to hand and no one to call. I ran to the other door on the balcony and opened it into another room. Another three came towards me, walking sideways, yet not advancing. The way to the outer door was blocked.

I looked towards the TV and the shelf beneath. The PlayStation still hummed. I had played the game too long. The images burned into my retinas.

Okay, what do you think to flash fiction? Whatever, there's more later. Meanwhile...

HEARING AIDS

I was in the hearing department of the local hospital. My GP had sent me for a hearing test. Never having been in this section of the hospital before, I presumed it would be like the other departments where one had to sit and wait, and wait, and wait. A few people knew each other, so I reckoned it was perhaps a regular meeting place. I was sitting near the back of the area next to an elderly gentleman.

'What time's your appointment?' he shouted as I placed my carton of coffee on the floor in front of me and spilt most of it with the sudden shock of his voice.

'Eleven,' I replied, in a quieter voice than his.
He jerked his upper body round to face me and stretched his neck.

'How long have they been doing evening appointments?' he replied, un-stretching his neck, and turning towards the front.

'Eleven,' I said, louder.

'You'll have to speak up, I'm a little deaf.'

If he's a *little* deaf, what am *I* doing here? He began fiddling with his hearing aid.

'Three years 'I've had this, and it's never worked properly.' He told me and everyone else in earshot, who grinned or giggled. 'Here, have you got one o' these types?'

He showed me the aid he'd removed from his ear.

'China! How do they expect them to work if they're making them in China?' He stood up and adjusted something in the front of his trousers.

I took a drink of my coffee and glanced around.

'Ahh, that's better,' he said sitting down. 'It's this new truss for my hernia – poor fit. Something else made in China. I don't know why everything has to be made in Korea or China nowadays, aren't we capable anymore?'

I looked at my watch.

'Have you been waiting long?' he said, as if I'd only just arrived.

I could hear tittering behind me and began to grin. I had to look away and took a deep breath.

'No not long,' I replied. 'Have you?'

'They'll be on their tea breaks. I was waiting three hours last time.' He continued, still fiddling with the hearing aid.

I hope I'm not going to be here as long as that, I thought, and took another drink of coffee.

'I don't know how you can drink that muck.'

I spilt some back in the cup and began to cough.

'See how harmful it is, you weren't coughing before you drank that, were you?'

A nurse suddenly appeared carrying a pile of folders.

'Mr Hemmings,' she called. She called again, louder and two men stood up. One man was in the front row, the other was the man now standing, next to me.

Looking at them both in turn, she called again.

'William Hemmings.'

The two men continued to stand and look around. The nurse walked over to the man at the front.

'What's your date of birth, William?'

'I'm not late,' he replied. 'It's you that's late.'

She asked again, speaking close to his ear.

'What's going on?' said my neighbour, looking around, agitated.

'You'll have to speak up. I'm deaf in that ear,' the man at the front said to the nurse.

Some of the people waiting couldn't contain themselves and had to leave the area. I too was finding it increasingly difficult not to burst out laughing at this occurrence in the hearing clinic.

Unperturbed, the nurse continued. 'Have you brought any papers with you, William?' He looked behind at his vacated seat and picked up the newspaper...

'No, William, official papers.'

'Has someone taken my place?' said my neighbour.

'I'm coming over to see you in a minute, sit down please!' shouted the nurse.

'But I haven't seen anyone yet.'

The man at the front pulled some envelopes from his inside pocket and handed them to the nurse. She glanced through them.

'Right, that's sorted, wait here.' Handing the papers back, she came over to my neighbour. 'So, you're William Hemmings as well?'

He stood up. 'I'm seeing Mr Flemming, aren't I? I don't want to see that coloured bloke I saw last time. Can't hear a word he's saying...' He looked around for support. I looked away, embarrassed as the nurse handled the situation.

'Let me check your identity, William.' He handed her an envelope. 'Your name's Jennings, William.'

'Yes, I know, that's who you asked for.'

CONTAINS PEANUT OIL

While we're on a medical theme, I had to collect a prescription for my neighbour. She had been having problems with her nose and the doctor had prescribed some ointment for her.

I was reading the usage instructions to her, when I noticed a warning on the label: CONTAINS PEANUT OIL. Now this got me thinking as to how peanuts and nasal treatments could be connected. After giving it a bit of thought, I was convinced I had solved the mystery. So, next time your child shoves a piece of Lego into one of his orifices and you have to rush him to the hospital, you might just be on your way to finding a cure for some disease or other.

Have you ever seen a movie where it's had such an effect on you, it keeps coming back into your head, and you never get tired of seeing that same movie again and again? Some people felt that way over *South Pacific* (going back a bit too far here, I think!), *The Sound of Music*, or *Phantom of the Opera*. For me, it was *Titanic*.

I never tire of watching this film and never once did I think I was anything like Kate Winslet. Unlike a girlfriend of many years ago, who, when we went to see

Pretty Woman, on leaving the cinema, asked me if she looked like Julie Roberts? Friend or not, I couldn't help but laugh.

Anyhow, *Titanic*. Anything to do with *Titanic* and I am interested. I've even been to the Titanic museum in Halifax, Nova Scotia and sat in an original deck chair from the ship. I was so engrossed with this film, I was disappointed when I couldn't see Jack Dawson's name on the list of fatalities on the museum wall. When asking the curator why, I was embarrassed to learn he was only a character in the film... I crawled away quietly.

There was another time when something similar occurred. I'd not been in the fancy dress business long before being inundated with costumes orders. As I mentioned earlier, the variety was tremendous, and of course, I had to have some idea as to where to begin.

As the current theme was for British Kings and Queens throughout the ages, I thought the best place to look would be the library. There was no internet access in those days, and so I asked our local librarian if they had any references to images relating to such. After finding me a book containing colourful pictures, I took it back to work, only to return it the next day as there were no pictures of King Arthur and Queen Guinevere! If you're like me and didn't realise, there's a clue in the previous article.

Here's a bit of gossip for you. I don't know how true this is, but when actor Roger Moore was on set with his female partners, he apologized beforehand in case he got an erection—and if he didn't! Oooweee.

HOW TO DISAPPEAR

As an illusionist – in a puff of smoke,
A liar would insist he didn't exist.
Superman would pick himself up in a bucket.
Jack will pop back in his box.
Should I just vanish?

Dressed in grey, dive into the angry North Sea.
Wear green in a field of unripened corn.
In my Godsuit, slither in sludge.
In white muslin, a mirage beneath the Sahara sun.
Or gilded in silver, slip under slashed ice.

Wear yellow and get lost in a maize maze.
Twirl, like a restless spirit through a cotton field
And whirl up to the sky on a cloud.
Come nightfall, I will ride a black stallion
Up into a starless sky.

POP STARS

We shout and scream with gestures obscene
To our teenage fans as they wave their hands,
We go crazy on stage 'cos we're all the rage
And parents get cross, but we couldn't give a toss
'Cos we're Pop Stars.

The TV and the press we so like to impress
So we spit curse and swear no matter who's there,
We drink, and we smoke and haven't got a hope
'Cos we're quite insane with our drugged-up brains
'Cos we're Pop Stars.

We cause havoc and disgrace in every public place,
Especially on tour– Bollocks to the viewer,
We like doing what we do and haven't got a clue,
About manners and respect and unprotected sex
'Cos we're Pop Stars.

THE GARDENER

I am tall, dark and I presume, handsome,
Having no mirror, I cannot be sure.
I tend the gardens on a large estate.
My clothing is modest, and not of my choosing

My days are spent alone, tending the flower beds
And the orchard – the place I love most. But I
Long for a woman, with sweet-scented skin,
Large rounded breasts and child-bearing hips

To bear all my sons. But she's not appeared yet.
The boss says, she will – when the time is right.
I have to believe him; there is no one else here.
Hush! Up in the orchard, what's that I hear?

I run with good speed and stand firm, my spade
Held aloft. A flurry of leaves falls from a tree.
Come out, show yourself. A figure appears
She moves towards me with open hand –
Where sits an apple.

TOP OF THE CLIFF

One cottage left at this far reach of land.
There were twenty, back then, and built
Of limestone, horsehair and whatever else
Was to hand. At the top of the cliff.

Even the horses struggled, as their shoulders hunched
And their backs sagged with the weight of their loads.
They'll stand for centuries, the seller said,
Back then.

For no one knew how cruel the Westerlies could be,
And gradually, slow by slow year, each home
With its secrets, crumbled and slid down the cliff side
And into the sea.

THE TATTOOED MAN

He walked through the gateway into the field beyond,
Steps slow of pace, faltering. He stumbled upon
A millstone, from a time long past, where he sat
Listening to the silence, and opened up a can.

The river flowed beside him, but no fish did he see.
Nor the blackened trees aflame in the setting sun.
He didn't see the blood soaked earth where the
Ghosts of fallen soldiers still walked the war-torn land.

He didn't hear their cries of pain or smell their disgorged
Bowels, their missing arms and severed legs, and photographs
Of loved ones clutched to a broken chest. The tattooed
Man looked straight ahead and pulled another can.

THE CROOKED SPIRE

Have you ever seen or heard of the church with the crooked spire? It's in Chesterfield, a town in Derbyshire some thirteen miles from Sheffield. Its full name is **Church of St Mary and All Saints, Chesterfield.** Predominantly dating back to the 14th century, the church is a Grade 1 listed building and is well known for its leaning and twisted spire, an architectural phenomenon.

The church is mainly medieval and built of Ashlar, which is finely dressed (cut, worked) masonry. The seventy-metre spire was added later, in about 1362. It is twisted 45 degrees and leaning nine feet and six inches (2.9 metres) from its true centre. The leaning was long suspected to be the result of the absence of skilled craftsmen, owing to the **Black Death** of some twelve years previously and therefore, it had insufficient cross bracing and was built of unseasoned timber.

It is now believed that the twisting of the spire was caused by the lead covering, as when the sun shines during the day on the south side of the tower causing it to heat up, this causes the lead to expand at a greater rate than the north side, resulting in unequal expansion and contraction. This was compounded by the weight of the lead: on the seventy-metre spire: there is approximately 33 tonnes of sheet lead.

There are numerous folklore tales as to why the spire twisted. The most popular belief is that a virgin once married in the church, and the church was so surprised that the spire turned to look at the bride, and continues that if another virgin marries in the church, the spire will return to true again.

Chesterfield's Crooked Spire

OVERHEARD IN THE HAIRDRESSERS

I was in the hairdressers a few weeks ago, and you know how the customers gossip as if they're in a private, confidential MI5 chamber! Well, I overheard a conversation between a young woman and her stylist. The young woman was telling the stylist about a new man in her life and went on to illustrate certain intimacies that would make a street girl blush.

The stylist, somewhat embarrassed, tried to make light of this very personal conversation. As the customer had said the man was an electrician, the stylist proclaimed that was why he 'turned her on,' and 'could light her fuse.'

As the cut finished and the hair dryer switched on, I could no longer hear this intriguing tale and, where it was going. But it made me think about other occupations and how they could relate.

These are a few of what I came up with; you may want to add some of your own.

HOW DO YOU DO IT?

Hairdressers do it with style
Shop Assistants do it while talking
Electricians do it to get turned on
Farmers like to watch it grow
Racing Drivers do it – too fast
Mathematicians do it as a rule
Bricklayers lay one at a time
Gardeners do it against a south-facing wall
Nurserymen – like to plant their seed
Seamstresses do it by hand
Gynaecologists do it through the letterbox
Yorkshire folk do it up hill and down dale
Pilots do it automatically
Nurses do it with care
Surgeons – wear rubber
Dermatologists do it and come out in a rash
Psychiatrists do it like crazy
Orators – talk about it
Authors write about it
Bakers like to feel kneaded
Actors do it to get attention
Australians do it down under
Divers like to take the plunge
Economists do it for the money
Firemen do it in the heat of the moment
Footballers score every time
Foresters like a clear patch
Golfers lose their balls
Lift attendants –do it going up and down
Librarians do it quietly

Roofers do it on top
Upholsterers do it to cover up
Photographers do it with a time lapse
Architects draw it out
Dentists do it by mouth
Dog trainers SIT to do it
Narcoleptics dream about
Astrologers know when you're coming.

ON THE PHONE

What about this for a mind-boggling phone conversation?

> 'Hello, are you there?'
> 'Yes, who's that?'
> 'I'm Watt'
> 'What's your name?'
> 'Watt's my name.'
> 'Yes, what's your name?'
> 'John Watt'
> 'John what?'
> 'Yes. Are you Jones?'
> 'No, I'm Knott'
> 'What's your name then?'
> 'Watt's not my name.'
> 'Well tell me your name then.'
> 'Will Knot'
> 'Why not?'
> 'My name is Knott'
> 'Knot what?'
> 'Not Watt, Knott.'
> 'What?'

***

A very funny conversation; I'd sooner deal with a call like that than an operator in a Delhi call centre. I have enough hearing problems without adding to them.

Nuisance callers, they're the best ones to get. I know how to deal with them now though. The conversation goes something like this...

Ring, ring.

'Hello.'

'Hello, Missees Cleek.'

'Yes...'

'Missseees Cleek,' Happy voice – got a hit. 'I am calling you today about your Sky televeesion and how you can rrreduce your payments.'

'Oh! You're ringing about the car?'

'Car? Ah, no, you meesunderstand, I am phoning about your televeesion.'

'No, you misunderstand, I spoke to you yesterday and you said you would ring back to...'

'No, Misseeess Cleek, you are meestaken...'

'Well it is three years old, and I know Barbie pink is not everyone's colour but...'

Click, buzzzzzzzzzzzzzzzzzz...

Here's another conversation...

GARDEN CONVERSATION

'Rose, Rose, our Lilian's been picked for the festival.'
I didn't reply. Lily was always bragging. I wonder
Why haven't I been chosen? I was far more beautiful

I don't like Lily or Lilian for that matter. Taller than I,
They stand opposite, across the crazy paved path.
Turning their heads to passers-by. Common as muck.

Flaunting, Nectar oozing. Garishly dressed, crimson,
Yellow, orange. Ivy turns to the wall when she sees them.
Mother called them brazen hussies.

Mother passed last week, cut down in her prime. I miss
her.
An aristocrat. Palest of pinks. Graceful, fragrant,
She always said she was too good for this place.

'Oh Hello,' Poppy's just arrived. She never stays long –
Prefers the Countryside. 'Sorry to hear about your
mother, Rose,
At least it was quick. Better than dying of thirst.'

I hear Iris is moving. 'Yes, she says it's like being buried
alive.
Too many of them sharing that one bed, if you ask me.'
'Yes, she does look a bit blue, not like me,

Give me a bit of sunshine, and I'll thrive anywhere.
Look out! Here comes the gardener's dog.
If he cocks his leg on me again...Argghh! Too late.'

'He doesn't do it to me anymore, got too near my thorns
Once, that stopped him.'
'Glad I'm not at the back with Gladys and Delphine,

75

He does far worse up there, by all accounts.'

'Here, what's that smell? Is it what I think it is? Ah!
Feeding time. Here comes old Sam, just look at that –
A lovely barrow-full of muck.

GOING HOME

They covered their ears as the C17 came into land. My hearing had long gone. We waited in line for the huge doors to open. We'd done our bit and were on our way home. Martin, next to me, hadn't spoken since that day, nor had I, come to think of it. I remembered the old timers who couldn't forget the horrors they had seen on the Somme, yet somehow, we knew. The carrier taxied, quietened and came to a stop, Bill Travis batting him in. I could see him now, his face covered in sweat; he couldn't stand the heat. God knows what he was doing in Bagram. We had no choice; we went where told.

The Globemaster's doors opened, and men and supplies rolled down the ramp. An hour had passed before the cargo was off-loaded and used equipment filled the space, our turn soon. We'd seen it all before. Another hour passed and John Bates arrived carrying his brass. The camp commander followed and said a few words. John placed the instrument to his lips. We began moving, nothing stirred, only the flags draped over our coffins.

CITY SUPERMAN

A man dressed as Superman was taken to Saint James hospital with multiple injuries yesterday.

Gordon Hill, who witnessed the incident and called the ambulance, said. 'He just stepped onto the main road and stopped the traffic, allowing an elderly lady to cross.'

Police Officer, John McNamara, said he couldn't believe the man was still alive and refused treatment from the paramedics, who assessed 'Superman's' injuries as severe.

The driver of the forty ton juggernaut, who couldn't avoid running into the man, was slightly injured and was taken to hospital, suffering from shock. The vehicle, with severe frontal damage, was towed away.

'Superman', who insisted he would fully recover in a couple of hours, was eventually taken away. Unsure of his mental stability after such horrific injuries, the doctor stated that he would be heavily sedated and placed in a locked room on the fifteenth floor, while the tests analysed him.

Two hours later, a team of shocked medics led by Professor Davies rushed to his room, saying the X-rays didn't develop and the blood tests proved to be non-human.

After unlocking the door, they found the room empty. The secured and barred window was open. CCTV footage from the corridor showed that no one had left or entered the room.

A police spokesman said they would like to hear from anyone who can give any information on this person or his whereabouts.

THE TEST

A splatter of rain fell on his head as he peered out; he would hide for a while. Taking a deep breath, he looked down at his chest, small muscles rising within. Not as dark in colour as his parents, but enough to give him the camouflage needed to blend in with his surroundings. He felt the strength in his legs and the power that would carry him over the vast terrain; turning his head, he listened: silence.

It was time for him to leave the family home and begin an independent life. His siblings had already gone, each on their separate journeys, and now it was his turn. They had come of age and were no longer protected by their parents, who had tirelessly fed and kept them warm and safe. The outside world was fraught with danger, and he knew that once he left, there would be no return; he too would become the hunted.

Light of weight and built for speed, his swiftness necessary for survival. His first task to prove himself would be to find food and water. His parents, who had fed their offspring well on a diet of meat and vegetables, would be close by ready to assess his abilities.

He looked out again. It was time; his sharp, dark eyes scanned the horizon. His quick young mind calculated the distance, and the skills that had been handed down were now honed and ready. Sharpening his weapon, he looked around; the rain had ceased, the air fresh and visibility was now clear.

Limbering up, he jumped up and down, hopped from one foot to the other and then came out of hiding. Visible to all, he halted; something or someone was passing. He took a step back. The white people. With shallow breaths and heart pounding, he stood unmoving hidden only by the shadow and waited. With the danger gone, he gave a quick look behind to see what had been his home for the last ten days, gave a shrill cry and leapt off the edge. His wings opened, and the last of the blackbirds left the nest.

THE ACCOMPLICE

'What are you crying for, Becky?'

'I wanted a proper sandcastle, Daddy.'

'Look, sweetheart, stop crying and pass me some more pebbles.'

'But it doesn't look like a castle.'

'Wipe your eyes, while I go and fetch some larger pebbles.'

'Don't leave me here, with no one else around.'

'Just do as I tell you, sweetheart.'

'But, Daddy?'

'What now, Poppet?'

'I didn't really mean it when I said I wished Mummy was dead. She wouldn't let me wear my sparkly pink bathing suit.'

'It's too late now, Becky, you handed me the spade, so that makes you an accomplice.'

FIRST CLUTCH

She had gone missing again. Why did she keep abandoning her eggs? The young female Mallard had left her nest for the third time. Her mate, on constant watch, saw her and gave chase. He had to get her settled. His plumage was dulling, and there were other unattached females available.

The place she had chosen was ideal, although quite bizarre. A few missing stones in the garden wall. Close to the river and protected from the elements. English Ivy tumbled over the gap, giving her mottled brown feathers and the flash of blue over her wings the perfect camouflage. Only the darker line across her eye was visible. This had to be her first clutch and she was unsure how to react, unlike the mature hens that nested on the riverbank. They laid an egg a day and apart from a few daily breaks for food, a swim and preening session, they remained until the ducklings hatched.

A week later, as she was on the lawn, I went over to her nest and I peered in. It contained three pale blue-green eggs, lightly covered with ivy, feathers and leaves. I looked the following day; another egg had appeared. This daily ritual continued until ten eggs had been laid.

She sat, turning them at regular intervals, carefully covering them before she ate and bathed in the river.

Almost a month after laying the first egg, within a twenty-four hour period, the eggs hatched. Next morning, Momma Duck flew down from her nest. Her young followed, nervously fluttering to the ground. I counted nine. She didn't wait, she didn't look back. She made her way across the lawn and down the steps to the river, the youngsters, tumbling in pursuit. I looked in the nest. Only one cracked egg remained.

COUGARS AND COUNCILS

I was off to a meeting: showered, dressed and make-up applied. Then realised I hadn't put any deodorant on. Looking in the bathroom cabinet, I found mine empty, so I used hubby's, Lynx Africa.

I gave a quick squirt under my blouse and into my armpits. Wow, I thought, pretty strong stuff. A quick look in the mirror told me I looked smart enough to meet the bookseller. Wearing my new trouser suit, heels, and carrying my briefcase, I left the house.

As I walked through the store, I noticed a lot of admiring glances from some of the males and felt quite pleased, *there's still life in the old cougar yet*. Until I discovered they were gay.

While I waited to see the manager, I bought a newspaper and began reading about the local councils, and health and safety blunders. As a rate payer, I too am concerned about the ridiculous amount of money they spend on rectifying blunders and supporting ridiculous schemes. No doubt you'll all remember the Icelandic Banks crash of 2008–2010 when approximately ninety British councils were affected, all having large amount of money invested with them.

Kent County Council had 50 million invested in Icelandic banks. The leader of the council at the time said: 'it had been a smart move.'

Less serious, but not for the persons involved, was the Norfolk family who were wrongly evicted, and someone's ashes being lost. Fancy having to explain that to bereaved relatives, plus the council had to refund the crematorium fee.

Another more recent council 'error', and by more than one council, was the illegal moving of bodies to cover up burial errors. They have been found to be 'sliding' bodies across in the ground instead of lifting them out. This is illegal, as disturbing bodies in consecrated ground must be formally permitted by a church court.

In 2015, I'll call him John Doe, was buried in the wrong plot, adjacent to the grave of another man who had died in 2012, who I'll call Jack Smith. But unknown to his family, John Doe's plot had been reserved for Jack Smith's son Ron Smith. The error meant that his father's dying wish for his family to be buried together could not be fulfilled.

When Jack Smith's daughter met the town clerk to discuss the situation, she was told that John Doe's body could be 'informally' moved sideways in the ground – a practice known as 'sliding'.

Another instance regarding the council, and one less serious, but not to the council officials, is in Chester. The council has removed a series of amusing plaques that had been added to park benches, claiming people could be offended by them.

The plaques were put on the benches by a group of street artists who said they had added them 'in good grace' and 'for the residents and visitors of Chester to enjoy while they can'.

One of the bench plaques read: 'This bench is dedicated to the men who lost the will to live whilst following their partners around the shoe shops of Chester.'

Another read: 'This bench is reserved for the young, beautiful and affluent. If you are old, ugly or poor please sit elsewhere.'

Among other plaques was one featuring the message: 'If you shut your eyes for more than 10 seconds whilst on this bench you may be deemed asleep, and risk facing an ASBO.'

Another declared a bench: 'The Homeless Inn', and advised 'Opening hours 22:00-07:00, 364 days of the year (Closed Christmas Day)'.

But council officials failed to see the funny side and have taken the signs down. 'We have removed the plaques as some people may find them offensive, and it has cost the council taxpayer money for officers to locate and remove them, 'said Maria Byrne, head of place operations for Chester Council.

I'm surprised they didn't throw another complaint in regarding Health and Safety laws which now seem to fill everyone with doom and gloom, even if they don't walk under a ladder. For instance – not only will some people find them offensive, some might tear their clothes if the plaque has not been professionally fixed. The message could be misinterpreted by someone with dyslexia or learning difficulties.

There used to be a programme on TV during the 70/80s, I think it was hosted by Esther Rantzen and called, 'That's Life'. She had a section where members of the public could send in suggestion nominees for the 'Jobsworth Gold Cap' award. This was intended to embarrass and name and shame any minor officials and bureaucrats, who were more concerned with political correctness and red tape above and beyond the call of duty. For instance, we've all had a letter demanding payment from the gas company, electric, water, whatever company, even though your home/business does not have a supply of the said utilities. And so you reply, either by phone or letter, taking precious time, only to receive another identical letter a month later.

Here's a little something I put together regarding council officialdom.

LOCAL COUNCIL DECLARES WAR ON FAIRIES

Our crackpot council is at it again, telling us what we can and can't do, just to make life easier for them and harder for the ratepayers.

According to our reporter, Norman Noesitall, 'The Council is introducing legislations, which prevent us from allowing fairy-folk into our gardens.'

Gordon Gobshite, a council spokesman said, 'Fairies, which can cause eye diseases in children and lameness in legless war veterans, are vermin, along with rats and pigeons.'

Denis Dickhead, Labour Councillor, said he was looking forward to the new amendments, as his garden was overrun with them, and suspects it to be the work of the Fight for Fairies or Tory Party.

Betty Clensall, remarked, 'This is a matter for the Department of Health. The fairy-folk have no form of sanitation. I have seen many of these fairy houses in gardens and play-areas, and none have any bathrooms or toilets.'

Harry Hectares, head of planning, followed up with: 'Any attempt to access the mains drainage system without a formal planning application will be severely dealt with.'

The Tory party candidate, Gordon Golddigger, laughed when asked to comment. 'The Tory party has more to do than favour fairies,' he said, as he lit a Cuban cigar with a diamond-encrusted cigar lighter.

Ted Noballs, Lib-Dem, refused to comment. Carson Garage, UKIP, said, 'Ever since we joined the EU, we have had nothing but trouble trying to keep them out.'

HOW YOU CAN HELP
- Sign the petition
- Be careful where you tread
- Use only Fairy Dust Fertilizer – Contact me for list of suppliers
- Make a wish
- Vote for me – Jack Jobsworth – at the next election

Here's a cheeky poem for you, hee, hee!

'HOME COOKING' – WHERE EVERY MAN THINKS HIS WIFE IS

But, she's not at home making pies, she's making eyes
At the butcher down the street – with the very large chopper
Who reveals it with pride as she lies on the block
Awaiting his...

Sausages, beef, pork or herb, tomato and curry,
Belly and top leg, oxtail and top-lift – 'Oooh do hurry!'
Big juicy meatballs and spareribs in a sauce of hot chilli
She moistens her lips at the size of his...

Fridge, where he keeps all his produce, pasties and pies,
Top rump and thick flank, fillet and neck, ham-shanks and
Ox tongues, game birds of pheasant, grouse and wild duck
With his guarantee of a jolly good...

Discount!

THE OTHER WOMAN

A sandwich, a trio, my husband and I are a threesome.
Together now for fifty years, us and his busty blonde.
I do not see her all the time, but when I do, she's on his arm.
She's been with him too long to part, he said. In fact
Longer than I. And that I knew of her when we wed.

But I was young and much in love and let her share our bed.
My parents caught a glimpse of her and didn't want to know,
But said instead, they wouldn't grieve for what they didn't see,
So out of sight was out of mind, that's how they dealt with it.
On holidays she came with us, but then it didn't matter,

Strangers, unknowns, unconcerned, they'd seen it all before.
My man and me, his busty blonde, sunning by the sea,
And nowadays it's commonplace, just look around, you'll see.

93

And when at last our time does come for a parting of the ways,
I'll take his hand in mine and many tears I'll shed, when
I look into his coffin and see his tattooed arm and she.

NAUGHTY MOLLY

While I was out,
Bit off my cat's ear and tore open her neck
Because it was raining and I wouldn't play ball.

When I returned, the house was quiet, too quiet
No furry bodies pushing around my legs
No cold wet noses sniffing in my bags.

Molly lay under the table, head low, unmoving
Tasha lay on her side in the middle of the room,
Unmoving.

I dropped my shopping and rushed to where she lay
The tiny bell on her collar rang as I held her to my chest
Molly cringed.

Pippa, my Patterdale, at the age of nineteen and
Oblivious to the happening, turned around on her bed
And slept-on.

Tasha, my birthday gift, now twelve years old
And spent her time sitting in the bay window or by the
fire.

I glared at Molly

'Molly, guilty, guilty,' I shouted, she looked away.
As I took out a needle and thread and stitched the
stuffing back in Tasha's neck.

***

*I wrote this after my seven-year-old Border Terrier did
this to my realistic-looking cat, which is of sentimental
value; my hubby bought it for me as I can't have a real
one owing to his asthma.*

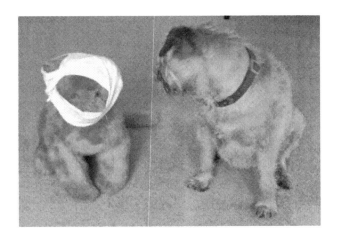

SUPERSTITIONS

Touch wood, say some, and knock on wood
White heather is lucky, and to see a black cat.
White rabbits, white rabbits, white rabbits
To be said on the first day of a new month.
Hang a horseshoe on the door – the right way up
Or your luck will fall out.
Don't walk under a ladder and there's seven years'
Bad luck if you ever break a mirror. No new shoes upon
The table, and never pass on the stairs.
Don't leave crossed cutlery on your plate or open
An umbrella indoors. Superstitious mumbo-jumbo
Legends, myths and lies, gibberish, gobbledegook.
I don't know whether to laugh or cry...
Oops! I've wrote 13 lines. I'd better add another, just for
luck.

A DIFFERENT CLICK

I click. Does that make me a clicker?
I don't walk any quicker.
And what of my click, does it grate on your nerves?
What purpose does it serve?
Does it torment your ears? And bring about fears?
It has soothed my tears.
So please get a grip. For when you hear me click
It's my new replacement hip.

Inspired by a South Korean Poem by Yi Won

FADING LIGHT

I am not an endless flame,
A money tree, an evergreen,
A mountain spring, eternal flow.
Now I am drought
With branches bare,
My light grows dim, too small to share
A spark, a pulse of light
Enough to make my world glow.

STONE CIRCLES

Endlessly marching
Around circles of stone
Sad figures move in shadows
Undying reflections
Soldiers lost in the field
Troubled, restless
Perpetual twilight
Left, right, left, right...
Circling the stones.

CATCH OF THE DAY

Dark River runs silently, with barely a ripple
Unseen, deep down he stays, skimming the pebbles,
Opportune feeding, mouth opening and closing
But not for the feast on my hook.

Tight lipped and determined, I cast yet again
For the prize-winning Barbel who senses my need.
My palms wet and clammy, anxiously gripping my rod
and reel,
Ready to haul him from out of his depth.

I cast once more with the non-tempting morsel
Into the domain of this beautiful Barbel. But he stays
there,
Unmoving...Waiting, 'till daylight fades to his favour,
Along with my hopes of the catch of the day.

Cold and disheartened, as I turned to leave...
There's a stirring, then a ripple, and a sudden darting.
Movement, of a whopping fifteen pounder, and a
glimpse of
Golden-copper, plunging back into the depths.

This is for any of you who have experienced sea-sickness.

STORM AT SEA

The sea will become calm, the good Captain said
As I fell onto the pillow and threw up in my bed.
I heaved yet again with the very next swell
As the vast ship rose, my guts lay where they fell.

You must eat, said the steward as he battled the door
And the contents of my stomach spread over the floor,
The ship rose again, and he disappeared,
As the hull rode the crest, he suddenly appeared.

The tray, still balanced on his hand held high.
'Leave me alone; I just want to die.'
Upon the table, he placed the tray
It slid straight off, taken by the sway.

The mountainous waves smashed into the ship
As she bucked and reared like a horse at the whip
Then shuddered back down to the depth of the swell
A storm at sea is another form of hell.

I DREAMED

Of sailors, sailing to an island.
Sailors, drunk on rum and dreaming
Of dark skinned girls with pearly teeth
And grass skirts swaying,
With long dark hair festooned with Orchids.
White sand coves and caves of darkness
Hidden chests of gold and rubies.
Ship gently rolling as they slept
Sailing to a land of plenty.

The following are poems I have written at different times and are linked to home and various happenings during my childhood in Owlerton, Sheffield.

IN THAT YEAR

My Grandmother died, I went to her funeral
But I didn't cry.
In that year and to the day the blackouts were lifted and mother gave birth.
In that year, Cousin Peter died with pneumonia
And I didn't cry.
In that year, after many attempts, my mother stopped smoking.
In that year, something happened in France and every one rejoiced.
In that year, Auntie Betty received a yellow telegram and never spoke again.
In that year, the coalman's horse dropped dead in our street
But I didn't cry.
In that year, I was born
And I cried

Attributed to Kim Moore

REMEMBER

Remember the cart we made with the wonky wheel
It trapped your foot and damaged your heel.
And the wooden sledge with solid steel runners
We painted it blue; it looked a stunner.
The boat we made which sank in the Don
Your brother was there. Otherwise we'd be gone,
The tree house with rope ladder way up high
We were the first to spy from the sky.
The shed we built to store our tools
Sharp and clean, they shone like jewels.
And then our first house – we thought it grand
Then went on to buy parcels of land,
From single dwellings to large estates
Blocks of flats, universities too
We've built them together – me and you,
What else? you ask, there's not much left
Apart from the final ultimate quest,
Our coffins, my friend, we will not build
Whoever does, I hope, is equally skilled.

THE JOURNEY

'Go forth to Britannia!' cried the great god Thor,
'A new metal has been found. It does not stain
Or even rust, I hear that sinks are made of such.
I'd travel too, were my eyes not dim, so alone
You must journey, son. Make haste, set forth before
The dawn and return with a stainless steel sink.'

'The seas are too perilous,' young Tyr replied.
To which his father rose. 'No son of mine shall
Fear the seas,' and ordered him to go.
At his father's command, young Tyr set sail
And braved the storm-filled sea, until at last
The waves did cease – Britannia, the far country.

Newcastle is where he came ashore and sought
The stainless sink. *'T'is coal we have here man,'*
The locals said. 'Sheffield's the place you need.'
So Tyr set forth on weary feet, for a hundred
Miles or more, and then, at last, the smoke he saw.
'City of steel,' he cried and ran the final score.

'I've travelled raging seas,' he said when he
Knocked on British Steel's door. 'A stainless sink
Is what I need, for my blind father, the great god Thor.'
'Tha's out o' luck,' the gaffer said after searching
Through his store. 'I'm sorry, son,' was his reply,
'We don't make 'em anymore.'

'Oh woe betide, what shall I do?' young Tyr did shake
His head. 'Just a minute,' the gaffer said and stroked his
Whiskered chin. 'Your father's blind, I heard you say,
I've something else that just might do, wait here awhile,
Please do.' So Tyr sat down with heavy heart,
Head resting in his hands.

105

Within the hour the man returned, in his arms a Builder's hod. 'Take this, young Tyr,' he said. 'It's free to you of course.' Tyr Jumped up with great dismay and shook his weary head. 'You mock me, sir, I can't take that.' 'Why not?' The gaffer swore. 'Have you never heard the saying, Tyr?'

'A hod's as good as a sink to a blind Norse.'

THE PURSE

'Quick, get the baby inside; the Gypsies are here.'
Said Mum and pulled in the pram from the yard.
I grabbed the baby and looked at mum as she
Quickly closed the door.

As old as she was she was fleet of foot, and
her hand held the frame of the door.
'Glass of water for a tired old Gypsy,'
she said, sitting down, unasked, on a chair.

Mum stepped back, and a filled a glass,
which she passed with a shaky hand.
Stale sweat and lavender hung in the air
as the gypsy slaked her thirst.

'Ahh! Tha's better,' the old crone said
and examined the crack in the glass.
Then patted her brow with a red and black
scarf and rustled her taffeta skirt.

'Thank ye,' she said as she wiped her lips
and stared with her smoke-black eyes,
'That's a bonny baby ye have there,' she said,
On her face a crooked smile.

Her dark eyes darted around the room
and settled on the shelf. 'Ye now buy pegs and
Lavender bags,' and reached down for her wares.

Afraid of her curse, Mum reached for her purse
and withdrew a silver bit, which she placed
in a thin woody hand.

'Ye've crossed my palm with silver; no darkness will visit
you.'
She returned the pegs to her woven bag
and rose onto bowed out legs,

Then came towards me and stroked my face;
I closed my eyes in fear; when I opened them
She had gone, along with mum's purse too.

STANLEY'S ORDEAL

My, you look smart this morning Stanley
You're just the lad I need,
Just slip down t'coal 'ole for us son
Our Ethel's lost our back door key.

I'll lift up grate while you climb down,
It's awful dark, don't slip on't sleck,
And mind them pans on t' cellar steps,
Don't want you to fall and break your neck.

You'll find a light switch on't back wall
Careful though, it's hanging off
And mind out where you put yer feet –
The's a mouse-trap there, which could go off.

What's that you say? The door won't budge
It will if you give it one good push,
One good shove now – ready, go.
WOOF, WOOF, GROWL, WOOF, WOOF

Stanley, you've gone and woke our Jake up,
Na don't be scared just pat his head,
He likes young boys – especially for breakfast –
Only jokin' Stanley, keep calm, he'll soon go back to bed.

Don't scream and shout or wave yer' arms,
You'll soon be on yer way
Move nice and slowly t' back door and fasten
Back the Yale. There now! Nothing to it. Eh?

Oh! Stanley what a sight y'look,
Yer mam'll murder you.
Come 'ere son
Take this penny and buy a sweet or two.

109

TIZER is a non-alcoholic drink launched in 1924, which became very popular during the forties and fifties.

I lived in Sheffield, just along the road from where this was made and bottled. During the Second World War, many women had to work in the factories doing the work of the men who were away. Much of the work was heavy, especially in the steelworks, but a bottling plant was hard work too. The glass bottles were large, thick and heavy, and so were the solid wooden crates which housed twelve bottles in each.

When the war ended, a lot of women were still necessary for the factories, as the returning men were needed to re-build the country.

I, along with other children of this era, was afraid of these heavy-set red-faced women and would wait by the factory gates for them to finish their shifts. As soon as the gates opened and we could hear the sound of their clogs, we would run along the pavement ahead of them shouting 'The Tizer Women are coming.'

This poem is in memory of the women who worked long hours at 'Pickup's' on Penistone Road, Owlerton, Sheffield.

'TIZER' WOMEN

Mothers, daughters, sisters, aunts,
With turbaned heads – crowns of their class...
Spew through the factory gates at close of shift.
Shoulders slumped from years of toil,
Their forearms crossed like mutton legs
Held tight against their heaving chests,
And red-raw hands shoved in armpits.

Leather aprons stained and wet
Bound around such hefty thighs,
Buxom girths sway with each stride,
And steel capped clogs spark every flag.
Haggard, hardened, old before time.
Skin the colour of the grimy brick streets,
Heavy-eyed they head for home

Where bailiffs prowl. And more demands.
Sick children cry, hungry husbands shout,
Aged parents moan of heatless fires
And foodless shelves. An empty purse
Such poor rewards for labours past
They can but hope, for a jug of 'mild.'
And a pack of 'Wood's' on Friday.

First published in 'The Girl with the Emerald Brooch'
Jacqueline Creek 2016

THE WEEK BEFORE CHRISTMAS

A time of frozen locks, non-starting cars,
Traffic jams and endless queues.
Freezing fog, black ice and snow,
Journeys fraught with choking fumes.
Shopping malls and car parks – full,
Shelves stacked with gifts and sold-out dolls
Faulty goods and lost receipts,
Harassed faces, aching feet.
Presents to get and cards to post,
Oh! Tracey's new baby – mustn't forget.
Prams and pushchairs, screaming kids,
Pushing, shoving, go with the flow,
Gifts to wrap, a tree to trim,
Fairy lights – must check the bulbs,
Tinsel, baubles and drawing pins,
Mistletoe and holly, wreaths for the dead.
Pies to make and cakes to bake,
Plus extra food – unexpected guests,
Whisky, Port and Sherry,
Fruit juice for the kids – oh!
That reminds me – Jackie's party
Gosh! It's fancy dress.

NEW YEAR

Another year has started, the other barely gone,
Yet Easter Eggs are on the shelves with unsold Christmas toys.
Magazines and papers are full of glossy ads, tempting us to travel
To warm and sunny lands.

We advance the clocks one hour, and officially its spring,
The days are getting longer, the birds begin to sing.
New season's growth is sprouting each day in growing warmth,
The miracle of nature as each new life is born.

May-Day Queens and Whitsuntide, parades and marching bands
Force springtime into summer, and sunny days abound.
Hot sticky nights and garden lights lure moths to certain death,
And long school hols that never end – until the nights draw in.

Woods and fields are spun with gold, summer fades,
Autumn takes hold and mellow moods embrace the land.
Cool nights return, sweet sleep descends.
And darker nights change evening pleasures.

Shops once stocked with summer toys, now have grisly ghoulish needs
Witches, devils, masks and gowns: it's haunting time, it's Halloween.
Bonfires blaze, loud bangers sound, rockets fly whooping from the ground.
As old Guy Fawkes burns to ashes, we know that winter is almost with us.

113

Christmas time again draws near, almost full circle, the end of the year.

Glittering decorations now fill the shops, shelves filled with gifts,

Parties all around. Carols and Pantomimes, Santa on his sleigh.

The clock keeps on ticking, the New Year comes around.

AS A CHILD

I had a friend who could sew her fingers together,
We watched enthralled, mesmerized.
John Cade's eyes widened, and his face turned green,
Then he threw up on Christine Smith's winter coat.

Later, when mum wasn't around, I opened her box and
With a needle and a strand of woollen thread, stabbed
My finger. Mum heard me scream and when she saw the
Blood, slapped me hard on the back of my head.

I screamed again. The tears welled up and rolled onto
My cheeks. 'But mum, when Jacqueline Campbell
Does it, she doesn't bleed, she lets us watch and charges
Us one penny. 'Well, more fool you,' said Mum.

With a corner of her pinny, she wiped away the blood.
Another corner wiped my snot filled nose.
But Mum, it hurts, I sobbed. She wrapped her arms
Around me and kissed my tear streaked cheeks.

SHEFFIELD 1950s

I come from sheep's heads, oxtails, tatties and mash,
Cowheel and tripe, chitterlings and bag,
Rotting apples for a penny and long sticks of
Rhubarb, in a sugar bag.

I come from a terrace house in a street all the same,
Two up two down, dirty red bricks with a cellar for coal,
Smoking chimneys, lav up the yard, tin bath on the wall,
Used only on Fridays, bath night for all.

I come from where drop-forges thud day and night,
plaster falls
From the ceiling, cracks in the walls, women give birth,
Old people die. Hammers ring for the newborn –
Toll for the dead.

Surrounded by steel works and when night fell, workers
Turned a blind eye as we quietly crept by
To scrounge coal and coke, and push it home
In an old pram.

I come from a city where smog filled the air; death crept
into houses
Young and old lived in fear, Bronchitis, Pneumonia,
Rickets, TB.
Polio and Diptheria –Many were taken when these
Killers appeared.

I went to a small school where I learned how to read,
write and
Add-up, and about History, where good men died in
great wars
So we could be free, we gave thanks in Sunday school
For their gallantry.

I learned of poor children, in faraway lands, we could
Buy a photo for a penny to provide food for a week.
Friendly policemen walked down our streets,
Ready to help – a tearful child, with a grazed knee,
old ladies, cross the road...

I come from a city...I no longer know.

There, I hope they've evoked some childhood memories
for you too.

BON VOYAGE

With over 300 plane journeys in my life's experiences, on one occasion during a sudden violent storm, I became locked in a toilet. I have flown on Concorde, business class on British Airways to New York, and been one of only six passengers on a jumbo jet from Manchester to Tenerife. I've even been to Hell twice, but only once to Heaven. Thinking back, it was warmer in Hell than in Heaven. The first time was in Grand Caymen, the second time, I was in Norway. As for Heaven, that was nearer home, Somerset.

On a two centre holiday in Yugoslavia, now Croatia, I travelled first-class, on an internal flight from Rovinj to Dubrovnic, where first-class then was the equivalent of any cheap airline of today. Second-class passengers, who were allowed to carry rabbits, live chickens and other undistinguishable animals in small cages, were seated behind us, with a thin curtain partition separating the two grades. Third class passengers stood at the back of the plane, holding on to hanging straps.

One of my most memorable journeys was to the Arctic Circle. Have you ever been? What an experience! Apart from having sea-sickness where the North and Norwegian Sea meet, it was an awesome event. It was midsummer, the 20th June.

Although I have seen many glaciers, fjords and bays on my travels, this was magnificent, and I felt I was truly at the end of the world. Two things strike you as you sail into the colder northern waters: the silence and the continuous daylight.

We were on a small ship, bigger than a tiny boat, but much smaller than the cruise ship behemoths that sail the oceans nowadays. As we sailed further north, we were accompanied by a school of Beluga Whales, their pearly white bodies swimming close to the sides of the ship with their distinctive protuberant heads lifting out of the water as if in greeting. They stayed with us for a few miles and then satisfied we were no threat, plunged into the depths.

The ship was the perfect size for getting where the larger crafts can't. Slowly approaching Magdalena Bay – speed limits operate in these protected areas – the silence was gently broken with the sound of ice splintering and crunching around the ship, as the captain steered a steady course for his sight-seeing passengers.

We were clothed in fleeces and anoraks, hoods tightly fastened, covering sensitive heads and ears, thick trousers and warm shoes or boots. Looking out at the vast landscape, our cameras and video recorders were busy capturing the breath-taking views, while the attentive Filipino crew, wearing body warmers, handed out mugs of beef tea, hot soup and Hot Toddies at midnight.

The surroundings were surreal as we looked out on a landscape that was mostly untouched by man. Glaciers broke away, exhibiting the most perfect shade of turquoise blue. Ice splinters caught the sunlight, exposing miniature rainbows in the light of the pale midsummer sun.

We went ashore at Longyearbyen on the island of Spitsbergen, the largest and only permanently populated island of the Svalbard archipelago in northern Norway. It is the world's most northern town, along with the church, post office, ATM, museum, airport and university: all the northernmost. It is also Norway's largest island, measuring some 15,075 square miles. It is also built entirely on stilts. All pipes for water, fuel and waste etc. have to be above ground, with snow scooters, bobsleighs and skis all ready and available underneath the buildings.

As we wandered through the town, the reindeers never moved, happily nibbling whatever was poking through the frozen earth. The two thousand or so people who live in such a remote location are either miners in the few remaining mines or work in the many scientific establishments.

We were told that it is illegal to die on the island. In 1917, a strain of flu hit Longyearbyen, killing a lot of people, who were then systemically buried. Many years later, someone discovered that the bodies in the cemetery were not decaying, and the influenza strain was very much alive. So burials in Longyearbyen are no longer allowed. Bodies do not decompose because of the permafrost, which ranges from ten to forty metres deep, and residents with terminal illnesses are flown out to Oslo. So if you think you're going to die – go someplace else.

As we re-boarded the ship, the welcoming crew once again handed out hot drinks, as we all chatted about the experience and shared our disappointment, as no one had seen any of the 3,000 Polar Bears that live around Svalbard. As the ship made ready to sail, a lot of the passengers who hadn't been sleeping because of the few days of continuous daylight made their way to the cinema. There was no film showing, but it was the darkest room on the ship.

I continued to look out at the view, trying to imagine what it would be like to live without daylight for four months. The sun sets each year on October the 25th. It officially returns on March 8th, when a week-long celebration is held to welcome the return of the sun. The entire town gathers at precisely 12:15 to await its arrival.

As the ship slowly made its way from the shore on our journey south, the icy midnight-blue water lapped the sides of the ship as she picked up speed. Would I return?

You bet I will.

Do you know? Humans walked on the moon before wheels were put on suitcases!

***

I think it's time for some more flash fiction. What do you think to it? My guess is you'll either love it or loathe it, or, you might be undecided. Whatever – here's some more.

THE END OF THE LINE

Ron tried to reel in his line. Something was on his hook.

'You've at least a fifteen-pounder there, Ron,' said his pal, Malc, as he put down his rod to watch.

Ron tugged at the line. 'Whatever it is, Malc, it's stronger than me.' The rod bent and shook.

The canal water was still, black and smooth, as other anglers placed their rods on the bank and went over to watch.

'Think it's a Barbel?' asked Tom.

'There's no Barbel in this part of the canal,' Brian Higgins replied, as Ron struggled with the rod.

'You've more than a Barbel on the end of that,' said his brother, moving closer.

123

Tom lit a cigarette and stepped back to enjoy the spectacle. 'Could be a shark,' he laughed and began humming the Jaws theme tune.

'That's not funny,' Malc snapped. 'My lad and his mates swim in here.'

'Well, sharks have been seen in the canal before.'

'He's right,' said Brian Higgins. 'They come up the river when the sluice gates are open.'

'Bloody hell,' said Ron, as he continued his battle.

'Sharks my foot, you've been watching too many Jaws films,' laughed Brian's brother. The others joined in humming the theme tune.

Something stirred in the deep water. Ron, now with Malc's help and strained arms, held onto the rod.

A supermarket trolley, full of rusty metal, appeared from out of the blackness. The two anglers dragged it to the edge; the others walked away laughing.

Malc, grinning, bent to pick up his rod as Ron eased himself down the bank to free his line. His foot caught in the debris. Malc turned and saw Ron's terrified face as he sank beneath the bloodied water.

PIE FACE

'You've eaten so many pies; your face has developed a crust.'

Norman looked in the bathroom mirror. Had she really said that to him? His skin was thick, pale gold in colour, dry and flaky. Shocked, he turned his face to the side and saw potato leaves sprouting from his ears. He screamed. They *were* potato leaves.

Covering his face with his hands, he remembered his grandmother's hands and clothes smelling of onions, bleach and carbolic. He sniffed under his arm pits. Agghhh! He could smell gravy.

Norman had stopped eating beef pies after his mother told him he was beginning to look like Desperate Dan, which he didn't believe until he found he could strike a match on his chin. So he began eating chicken and mushroom pies instead. Flexing his arms, he saw beneath the tiny muscles, wings of flesh and feathers. He placed his foot on the toilet seat and looked at his toes. Mushrooms were growing between them. He tried to remove his trousers but his hands were now pigs' trotters.

'What's happening to me?' he cried. As he managed to drag his trousers away from his expanding body, he saw a stick of rhubarb and two apples between his legs.

Closing his eyes he screamed. On opening them, pies surrounded him. He covered his head and ears. Pork pies, meat and potato, chicken and mushroom, apple pies, rhubarb pies, danced around him chanting: *PIE FACE, PIE FACE, PIE FACE...*

'Norman? Norman? What on earth's the matter?'

He could feel the pies pulling at the covers over his head and face. 'No! stop it!' he called.

'Wake up, Norman, your tea's ready. I've baked a nice apple and rhubarb pie for you.'

'Agghhh!'

SEAFARERS

'Not be long before the new ship's ready, Chris. It's looking well, don't you think?' said Harvey, as he placed his quill pen on the leather top desk.

'Yes, it's coming along much faster than expected,' Christopher replied, lifting his hand from the parchment drawing on the table. He looked through the small crazed-glass window to where his new vessel was taking shape.

The shipwrights and engineers toiled endlessly. There would be severe penalties if it was not finished in real time.

''As her Majesty chosen a name yet?' Harvey asked, as he stood, straightened his doublet and reached for his clay pipe.

'Yes, the Pinta,' Christopher replied and looked up, as the office door opened.

'Excuse me, Sir,' said a young apprentice as he peered around the mahogany door.

'Step forward, boy and state your business,' snapped Harvey, annoyed at the intrusion.

The boy stepped nervously into the room. 'It's the Captain, Sir – he would like to see you as...'

Christopher raised his eyebrows as he looked at the youth, his breeches far too tight for respectability. A codpiece should be part of his attire at his age. He glanced towards Harvey.

'Tell him I'll be along shortly,' he said as he turned towards the window.

The messenger's eyes widened. 'But Sir, he said it was urgent.'

Christopher pressed his fists on the window sill and without turning said. 'Tell Pugwash, I'll be the keeper of timescale, not he'.

NEVER ASSUME THE BOSS KNOWS EVERYTHING

'I've put the new engine drawings and specification on your desk, Mr. Marshall,' Carol said, as she was leaving.

'Thank you, Carol. The Japanese company are looking forward to seeing the new design at tomorrow's meeting.'

'I'll be sorry to miss it, Mr Marshal, I know how important it is for you, but I'll be sunning myself in Majorca.'

'Lucky you. What time's your flight?'

'Nine o'clock tonight – must dash.'

'Have a good time, see you in two weeks.'

'Bye, good luck for tomorrow.'

My secretary closed the door as she left. I looked out of the window at the view. The rain poured down the panes. Streaks of black, red, white and yellow, distorted by car headlights transformed the scene into an abstract painting. My thoughts turned again to tomorrow morning's meeting. I returned to my desk, picked up the phone and pressed a button.

'Hello, darling, I'm just checking if everything is in time for tonight.'

'James, dear,' came her throaty reply. 'When have I ever let you down?'

'I'm just over-anxious – you know what this sale means to me.'

'Now stop worrying, you're the best person for the deal. Ferguson would never have given you the undertaking if he thought otherwise.'

I tapped my pen on the pad as I listened. 'Did you manage to acquire the Royal Suite?'

'Yes. Now get a move on, we're meeting the visitors for dinner at eight o'clock.'

'Yes, darling. See you later, bye.'

Tonight's dinner with the Japanese delegates was just as important as the meeting in the boardroom tomorrow. I pulled the sheaf of papers and blueprints towards me, looked them over and signed the appropriate documents. I re-stacked them and pressed the intercom. There was no reply.

'Blast.' I'd forgotten Carol had left early. I needed copies, and she wasn't here. I picked up the papers and went into the main office. Empty. Then I heard a noise over in the corner and saw a youth operating the machine. I walked towards where the sound was coming from; the young man went into another office. I looked at the apparatus, trying to find the correct buttons, when the youth reappeared.

'Hello there,' I said. 'Do you know how this machine works?'

'Yes, sir,' he replied.

'Thank heaven for that. What's your name, boy?' I handed over the documents.

'Robert. Robert Parker, Sir,' he replied.

'These documents are highly confidential, Robert. Can you see to them, please? I have an important meeting and must be on my way.' The youth began feeding the papers into the machine.

'I'll just get my briefcase and come back for the copies,' I said and turned towards my office.

'But Sir,' replied Robert, as the last of the papers disappeared into the machine. 'This is the shredder.'

SMOKE SIGNALS

The young Indian Brave ran into the elder's tepee.

'Running Bear, come quick, there are smoke signals over Black-Foot's land.'

'Slow down, Crazy Horse. The spirits have taken my running powers. I can no longer walk with haste.'

Running Bear made his way to the entrance flap and looked out over the Great Plains; he raised his hand to shield his eyes from the glare and looked at the pillows of white smoke, rising into the sky.

'What does it say?' Crazy Horse asked.

'We must tell the chief of this.' Running Bear looked at the youth and began walking as fast as his legs would allow. The young brave followed, wishing the elder had more speed as they made their way to the chief's tepee.

Running Bear peeked through the flap, and looked at the boy.

'We cannot enter yet. Great Buffalo is meditating.'

While waiting outside, Crazy Horse walked around, admiring the war trophies festooned on the skins which formed the shelter, along with paintings of his tribe's great battles. He wondered when his time would come to join the war party. His eyes wandered to the central area, where the squaws were nursing babies and grinding corn or stripping hides. He was tired of waiting.

'Why can't we enter yet, Running Bear?' he asked, his bare feet kicking into the sandy earth.

'Patience, Crazy Horse. Great Buffalo knows we are here.'

A few moments later, the flap opened and they were allowed to enter. The young brave had never been in the Great chief's home before. He looked around at the buffalo hide walls. Wolves' heads and bears' feet, spears, tomahawks and scalps, all the chief's prized possessions hung as mementoes of his illustrious past.

The chief raised his hand in greeting.

'What brings Running Bear and Crazy Horse to speak with Great Buffalo? 'His voice was deep and coming from a cavernous chest, covered with a heavily beaded buckskin shirt, adorned with braids and animal and human teeth. His matching buckskin trousers were embellished with horse and human hair down the outer legs.

Crazy Horse stepped back, keeping hidden behind the elder. His eyes observed the sharp features of the chief's face, the well-marked cheek-bones, thin lips and aquiline nose, with keen black eyes sunk deep in their sockets, his long grey hair held back with a woven headband.

'Sit.' ordered the chief, and the two visitors sat cross-legged opposite him. 'Smoke first, then we speak.'

He turned and reached for his pipe which was on a table; a feathered war-bonnet stood in the centre.

Crazy Horse tapped the side of his foot on the ground; Running Bear nudged him and glared. The chief lit the pipe with a taper, which he then dropped into a small central fire. After three puffs, he handed it to Running Bear who did likewise and passed it to Crazy Horse, who took his turn, coughed and gave it back to the chief.

'Now we talk,' Great Buffalo said and patted his chest with his fist.

Running Bear patted his chest and spoke. 'Crazy Horse has seen smoke signals over Black Foot's land and wishes to know of its purpose.'

The chief looked across at Crazy Horse. 'You cannot read smoke?' He stood up and made his way to the exit; the two visitors followed him.

Looking out with his hand shielding his eyes, he watched the smoke for a few moments.

'Hmm.' He turned to the visitors. 'Black Foot's land two moons ride. 'He pulled open the flap and entered his tepee. Running Bear and Crazy Horse waited outside until Great Buffalo re-appeared and stood with his arms folded across his chest, wearing his war-bonnet. Crazy Horse jumped back; the chief's face was painted with red, white and black paint.

'Saddle the horses.' Ordered Great Buffalo. 'And round up the Braves.'

Crazy Horse screamed and began dancing around in a circle, stamping his feet into the dusty earth, tapping his mouth with one hand as he hollered out the war cry and patted his hip to a rhythmic beat with his other. His lower limbs were no longer visible in the dust cloud. He pulled a tomahawk from his belt and lifted it high above his head, and swung it up and down with short hacking movements while nodding his head in unison to his continuous chant.

Great Buffalo stepped forward and snatched the tomahawk from his hand.

'Stop that.' He threw the tomahawk to the ground. 'Go. Get the braves and the squaws. Tell them to prepare for a journey.'

With face and body covered in red dust, Crazy Horse looked at the chief, a puzzled look on his face.

'If we do battle, why we take squaws?'

135

'Who said we go to war?' The chief replied. 'Black-Foot having barbecue and it's fancy dress.'

THE MISSING LINK

The vault reeked of damp and cold as the archaeologists broke into the tomb. Mathews gagged as the stale air filled his lungs. Johnson stared, his face blank. Blake and Collins looked at each other.

'You'd better get the professor,' said Mathers as he backed away from the empty tomb.

The Arab helpers waiting in the background sensed something was wrong and mumbled to each other in their own language.

Collins ran up the ladder. 'Professor Heinkel,' he called on reaching the top, his eyes squinting with the sudden change of light. 'The tomb is empty.'

Professor Heinkel wiped the sweat from his brow and turned as he heard Collins' voice.

'It's what?' he said as he ran towards the dig, a look of shock on his face. He wiped the moisture from his glasses and replaced them. Both men stumbled down the ladder to the empty tomb.

'It looks like someone has beaten us to it,' said Mathers. The stale air dispersed and was replaced with a shaft of light from the Cairo sun. The men raised their helmets and dabbed their heads and necks.

Professor Heinkel entered the empty tomb; his all-seeing eyes scanned the roof, floor and walls. His eyes remained fixed on the wall. He took a step nearer and wiped his glasses again. The men kept quiet, wondering what the professor was thinking.

Collins, frustrated by the silence, said: 'Well?' Heinkel ignored him and moved closer to the wall. He stopped in front of a faded panel of hieroglyphics.

'All the treasure and the sarcophagus has gone, Heinkel,' said Collins, shaking his head.

'Perhaps not,' replied Heinkel. He took a small brush from his belt and flicked it over part of the wall. 'If this is what I think it is, it's worth more than the entire contents of the Valley of the Kings.'

He turned to face them, his eyes sparkling.

'Gentlemen, I believe we have found something remarkable.'

The men closed in. He turned and brushed more of the wall, uncovering more of the strange faded symbols.

'What is it? I've never seen hieroglyphics like this before.' said Collins, as he examined the wall. He removed his helmet and scratched his head. Mathers also looked confused.

'What language is this?' He looked at Collins, who stared back, bewildered. The Arab helpers began muttering quietly amongst themselves.

'My God!' Professor Heinkel suddenly called out as he turned towards his colleagues, his usually tanned face now pale and in shock. He sat down on one of the packing crates. The archaeologists moved closer and looked at the meaningless images. Only the professor knew the meaning of this mystical language.

Collins, agitated, shook Heinkel by the shoulders.

'You must tell us, Professor, now.'

The professor took a deep breath and looked at each of them.

'Gentlemen, prepare to be shocked. I suggest you take a drink of water.'

Anxious glances passed between the men as they unfastened their flasks.

The professor stood. 'These Glyphs, gentlemen are pre 3000 B.C. This is the missing link the world has been waiting for.'

The men gasped and stared at the wall.

'Many years ago, I dreamed of a find like this. Of course, all the tutors and experts said it would be impossible. There was a great void before 3000 B.C. But

139

I was certain there had to be more. Every spare hour, I looked into it but it was like searching the universe. With every avenue unproductive, I gradually accepted the fact that I would never find an answer. But my mind, all those years ago, had photographed those earlier glyphs, and now, when I see this...' He pointed to the wall. 'Those early images came flooding back, and this, gentlemen, is a priceless revelation, the missing link. And only I know its meaning. Gentlemen, what I am about to tell you now...'

A shadow passed over the entrance to the tomb and one of the helpers ran up the ladder. The professor, stood. A flash, followed by a dull thud, echoed around the chamber. The men jumped back as the professor collapsed to the floor, a red stain spreading across his jacket, his eyes wide open.

The tomb immediately filled with Arabs holding rifles, their heads covered with Keffiyehs.

'Treasure,' one of them screamed. 'Where is the treasure?' He fired the AK47.

The team swiftly raised their arms.

One of the helpers who had been on the dig pointed to the wall.

'Is that where the treasure is?' He pointed his rifle at the helper. The helper nodded.

'It's through there,' the leader shouted to his men and nodded them forward.

'No!' cried Collins and Mathers, as the raiders took aim and fired repeated rounds at the wall.

21ST OCTOBER 1966

'Do you want to know? Well, I'll tell you. I'll never forget that fateful day: it will hang over me till the fields fail to turn green. One hundred and sixteen children lost their lives, along with twenty-eight adults. Taken by an act of God, said some, but I knew different.'

I shook my head as the memories flooded back.

'We dug and scraped until our fingers and nails bled. We worked as a team, an unstoppable labour force.'

'Are you all right? Here, let me get you another drink.'

My chin sank to my chest as I recalled the sudden silence and then sudden rush of terrifying sounds, like a plane about to crash.

'I got you a large one, I thought you needed it.' He placed the pint glass on the table.

'Thanks.' I drank through the creamy top to get to the bitter ale beneath. Taking a large draught, I wiped my top lip on the back of my hand and continued.

'It was quarter past nine in the morning, when over a hundred and fifty thousand cubic metres of saturated debris broke away and flowed downhill at a terrific pace. It slammed into the village, a slurry twelve metres deep, destroying a farm and twenty terraced houses before finishing in the junior school and part of the senior school. It destroyed most of the structures, filling the classrooms with thick mud and rubble up to ten metres deep.'

I took another drink while I collected my thoughts. The reporter remained silent, waiting.

'There were faint cries and screams, and then silence before another sound filled the air – the cries of parents, shouting and screaming, running towards the school. The air was so dirty and thick with damp slag dust, I can still taste it. Hundreds of miners came from nearby pits and from further afield; carrying picks and shovels, in open-top lorries.' I looked at the reporter and took another drink.

'Because of the awful conditions, it took almost a week to recover all the bodies.' I looked down at my lap, the palm of my hand pressed to my forehead. 'I was one of the lucky ones. My children were in the unaffected part of the senior school. But it didn't stop me giving my all, and life if need be, to save just one of the poor mites from suffocating in such a grim death.' My eyes filled with tears and my voice caught in my throat. I shook my head.

'Do you want to stop?'

I raised my head. 'No, I'll carry on.' I sat for a moment. 'Then, when all hope had gone, it was a time of acceptance and haunting silence, apart from the never ending sobs of great grief from those who will never find solace. Days ran into weeks and months, but the valley had changed, it would never be the same again, ever. Some wanted to stay, near to where their loved ones had perished, others wanted to leave and never return. Then of course, there was the reckoning. The National Coal Board, in complete denial, stated nothing could have been done to prevent the slide.' I finished my drink and placed my hands on my knees, ready to leave.

'And yet, you still live here?'

'Yes I did not need to leave. I shared their sorrow.'

'Did it affect your children in any way, losing their friends in such a tragic way?'

'Children get over grief far quicker than humans, they move on.' I stood, and took a deep breath. 'My two boys left school the following year to go to college in Birmingham. They were killed in a coach crash in Pontypool before they left Wales. Twins they were.'

BODY LANGUAGE

He came from out of nowhere. I raised my club, and so did he. We stared at each other. Two drenched figures, crouching warily. Wooden clubs in hand, our hair hung in matted strands. The wet animal fur covering our bodies reeked of damp, musk, earth, and old bodily fluids. We raised our heads, trying to sniff the source of the other's scent. We could tell if the skins we wore were from an area other than our own.

Lightning struck, illuminating the sparse and desolate landscape. Thunderbolts rolled in, the noise cracked and thumped in our ears. Our eyes remained fixed on each other.

'Huh,' he grunted, his dark eyes set deep beneath a thick brow.

'Guh,' I replied.

We sniffed again, collecting each other's scent, slowly walking around each other, fearful yet aggressive. Ready to attack and kill if necessary.

'Gru,' he growled and raised his voice and club. I remained silently watching, my nose twitching.

The lightning struck again. The mountains and the ground beneath us groaned. Rain poured down from a sky almost the colour of night. Within seconds, earth, dust and debris collected in the streams; rivers formed. Shrubs and trees were uprooted as the water swallowed the land. Steam and smoke lay in its wake.

He moved closer, larger than I. He knew this was to his advantage. Nevertheless, he had every reason to be wary. I could jump on his back, gouge out his eyes and slit his throat with a sharpened stone before he could shake me off. Men were slow and lumbering. Sometimes it was advantageous to be small.

He raised his club again and took a step nearer. I backed towards my cave. A split opened in the earth between us, belching out smoke and lava rocks. I turned and ran, but he leapt over the gap. Stumbling into my den, I turned, threw myself at the boulder and pushed with all my strength. Loud cries erupted from his throat as he struggled to free his trapped arm.

Feeling around in the darkness, I found my sticks and flint and made a fire. My food supply was sparse. Only the bones of the sloth I had eaten yesterday remained, its skin hung on the wall to dry. I found a few berries and grains and cupped my hands beneath the trickle of water running from a crack in the wall. As I moved back towards the stone, I listened and peered through the small gap along the edge. He was still there, moaning and bleeding from his injuries. Now I could sleep. If he were dead by morning, I would have meat. I sharpened my stone knife, then placed more wood on the fire and lay down on the pile of skins.

Morning came, and I awoke to the sound of thunder, and pouring rain. A glimmer of light shone through the small gap. I listened, and then peered out. He had gone. Had he been dragged away during the night by some hungry beast, or had he recovered and lay in wait? I tucked the knife into my sinew belt, picked up my club and moved towards the stone. I listened again; there was only the sound of the rain and the distant cry of an animal being devoured by another. I pressed my back against the boulder and stopped. What was that? I waited and then pushed again; the gap opened. A hairy hand grabbed my wrist.

He forced himself against the stone, opened the gap and entered my cave. My club fell to the ground. I grabbed my knife, but he caught my other arm, bending it back at the wrist until I dropped the knife. I sank my teeth deep into his hand.

'Arh,' he cried, and threw me to the floor, away from the knife and club. I grabbed a stick from the dying fire and rushed at him. Pushing me to one side, he picked up my weapons and looked around the cave. Hanging on his belt was a freshly killed fox. He threw it towards me.

'Huh,' he said, then turned and left.

I looked at the fox and ran after him. 'Guh, gah,' I called, and raised the fox up in the air, making slashing movements with my other hand.

He walked back towards me with club raised and passed me the knife.

The skinned and gutted fox was roasting over the fire when he returned, his injured arms full of wood and kindling. I jumped up and grabbed the knife. A clap of thunder rolled across the sky, shaking the ground, and another split in the earth appeared, filling the cave with dust and smoke. Choking, we ran to the back of the cave and crouched, waiting for the tremor to pass.

'Aga,' I said, and pointed to the fox, which had fallen into the fire.

He jumped up and with a stick, lifted it back onto the wooden spit, then sat cross-legged watching it. I sat opposite, the roasting meat between us, our mouths watering. A leg fell off the fox into the fire; he scraped it towards himself with a stick, rolling it around on the floor to cool. I ran to where the fox leg was and grabbed it. He snatched the meat from my hand and pushed me away, then knocked the rest of the roast off the spit.

'Aga,' he looked at me and pointed to it.

I crawled over and ripped a leg from the carcass.

'Mmm,' I pulled at the coarse, hot meat with my teeth and swallowed it quickly.

Ignoring the intense heat, he held the flesh to his mouth, tearing off and swallowing great lumps of the grisly meat. He tore at another leg.

'Mmm,' he mumbled as the juices spilled out of his mouth and down his hair-covered chin.

I finished before him and wiped my hands across the stitched skins covering my chest.

Content from the food, I leant back against a rock and looked at him. The blood on his forehead, arms and in his hair had dried and turned black. His eyes met mine; I gave a faint smile.

'Dah, guh,' he shouted, jumped up and pulled back his lips, baring his teeth.

My body stiffened; he was angry. 'Keh, ghi,' I said, and raised my empty hands.

He gave a loud belch.

I stood up. 'Wa.'

He tucked the club under his arm and watched as I walked over to the trickle of water, I cupped my hands under it and drank. 'Wa,' I nodded. 'Wa.'

'Wa,' he said, and drank.

A flash of lightning struck followed by another rumble of thunder. Rocks and dust fell from the roof of the cave. The land shook and tipped, throwing both of us to the ground. We lay curled, with our arms and hands over our heads, until the earth stilled, then slowly rolled over. My covering tore as I turned.

Moving each limb, we checked for damage. Bruised and grazed, we looked at each other. His eyes widened as he saw my breasts. Licking his lips, he reached out; his rough, coarse hands grabbed hold.

I shuffled backwards, away from his hair-covered arms and tried to stand, but he grabbed my ankle and pulled me towards him. He raised the edge of his garment; his member sprang forward, large, hairy and erect. Saliva ran down his chin. Twisting my body around, I tried to scramble away, but he made another grab and ripped off the remainder of my covering. I was naked and on my knees. He tucked an arm under my belly and pulled me beneath him. Trapped between his thighs and his weight, I was helpless. With his hands firmly on my hips, he forced himself into me.

'Hmm, huh,' he grunted and urged his body backwards and forwards. The more I struggled, the more excited he became. He groaned, thrusting his pelvis deeper. After a while, something in my loins stirred. I grew aware of his strength and my weakness and began to enjoy the movements.

'Huh, huh,' he grunted again, holding me tightly beneath him. I soon fell into the rhythm.

His movements became faster; then he suddenly jerked, and his body stiffened. He collapsed down on top of me. 'Uhh, uh, uff, hck...FUCK!'

EUREKA! The first four-letter word.

I'm getting hoarse with all this talking, so before we move on, I'm going to make a cuppa. Here are a few medical notes for you to ponder on while I'm gone. I learned about these during a recent stay in the hospital. And no, it wasn't the consultant, doctors or nurses who told me. I found this info in the library.

MEDICAL NOTES

The heart is a muscle which never tires. Over a lifetime of say, seventy years, it will beat 2.5 billion times without taking a rest.

One single drop of blood contains 250 million red blood cells, 375,000 white cells and 16 million platelets.

One adult's blood vessels, unravelled and outstretched would encircle the earth twice.

Oxygen carrying red blood cells make up 99 per cent of all blood cells. Every second, 2 million new red blood cells are made by jelly-like red marrow inside our bones.

The largest artery and vein (the aorta and vena cava) each as broad as a thumb, are 2,500 times wider than a capillary which is just one-tenth the width of a hair.

Amazing eh? I wonder who counts all this stuff.

BEYOND BLING

Right, cup of tea downed. I have to tell you about this. I was inspired to write this poem after seeing a jewellery exhibition by Marjorie Schick. You'll have to Google her name to see more images as they are copyrighted. Her work is so bizarre, I've never seen anything like it and I began to wonder who would wear it, especially the dowel neckpiece...

Picture from www.artjewelryforum.org
Marjorie Schick, Arzo Orange 1986, necklace, wood, paint.
Photo: Gary Pollmiller.

'Elizabeth, you cannot wear that, it's a preposterous idea.'

'Oh Philip, don't be such a boring old fahhhrt. Just because I'm ninety doesn't mean I have to dress accordingly.'

'I'll not allow it Elizabeth. You will look ridiculous in front of the president.'

'Philip, remember your position. You can't state what I may, or may not do. The President and his wife will like my new tribal ideas; it will take them back to their roots.'

'I have never heard of anything so outrageous, Elizabeth. What will Charles and Camilla think?'

'Oh come on, Philip, those two are more elderly than I. I need to change my image. Jewels, crowns, tiaras are no longer my style. I suppose I could have an image of a crown tattooed on my shoulder though. It would do you good to change as well. I saw a delightful spent match tie pin at the exhibition that would suit you.'

'So that's how you see me...a spent match?'

'Of course not Philip...More like a dead crow.'

Sign outside Reglas de la Casa, a wonderful restaurant in Cozumel, Mexico

HOUSE RULES

No Smiling, grinning, laughing

No Looking around

No Chewing with mouth open

No Gawping

No Foot-tapping

No Spitting

The sign was only written in Spanish and English! Obviously the worst offenders, but inside the staff and atmosphere was excellent, along with the meal – and wine.

Salut, José Here's a poem I saw on a board outside the Alex Restaurant, in Cancun, Mexico.

Bacon is red
Steak can be blue
Poems are hard
Eat here.

LIVE DANGEROUSLY

Have you ever been to Lanzarote in the Canary Isles? Isn't it a fantastic place? Ignore the black sand beach; it's Timanfaya National Park that I found fascinating. Walking on an active volcano, hot under the feet, if you push a stick in the ground, it will catch fire; pour water into a hole and make an instant geyser. Wow! Live dangerously.

A restaurant situated within The National Park, El Diablo, is noted as the most dangerous restaurant in the world, where steaks, fish and chicken are cooked on volcanic rock heated by the lava underground. The chefs preparing the food have to wear specific hardwood clogs to protect their feet from the heat.

There is much more to see in Lanzarote, especially the Jameos del Agua, a series of volcanic caves developed into 'the most beautiful nightclub in the world', fusing art and nature, complete with blind cave crabs. The auditorium is used for classical concerts and has perfect acoustics, and the Jameos has a turquoise blue swimming pool, where only the King of Spain is allowed to swim. All well worth seeing if you've never been before.

Another place that should be on your bucket list is Pompeii and Herculaneum, and there's time enough to see them both on the same day. Pompeii is more crowded than the latter and not just with tourists. Sadly there are a lot of stray cats and dogs that have made it their home, and I found it most upsetting. There were no shops or café where you could buy food to feed to them.

Beware of con-artists though. For instance, there was a long queue for the toilets, and as I moved nearer to the front, I could see a local chap selling sheets of toilet paper. Women had queued a long time, and some had to leave the queue to find someone who had some small change in euros. I gave my last couple of cents to the lady in front of me. When it was my turn; I snatched a roll of paper from him and marched into the toilet. He shouted something I couldn't understand, but I ignored him. When I got inside the toilet block, an old lady sat on a stool handing out two pieces of paper to each person, a large collection bowl on a small table by her arm. Probably the paper seller's mother.

We moved on to Herculaneum for the afternoon, which is much quieter and less crowded. There was less to see overall, but more in depth, as it is one of the few ancient cities that can now be seen in much of its original splendour. Unlike in Pompeii, the pyroclastic material that covered Herculaneum preserved wooden and other organic-based objects such as roofs, doors, beds, food and even 300 skeletons.

The following day, we visited Mount Vesuvius, and as I walked around the crater rim, my nose full of the smell of sulphur, I tried to imagine the horror of its most famous eruption, which took place in 79 A.D., and buried Pompeii under a thick carpet of volcanic ash, killing two-thousand people.

Mount Vesuvius spewed forth a deadly cloud of tephra and gases to a height of 33 kilometres (21 miles), ejecting molten rock, pulverized pumice and hot ash at the rate of 1.5 million tons per second.

Oooh! And to think I've walked around the crater rim.

Here's a poem I wrote following that visit.

THAT DAY

First we heard thunder and then the earth shook
The mountain trembled, angry, a festering boil.
We stood in shock, afraid and looked to the sky
A rolling darkness covered the morning sun
And within the hour, was dark as night.

Crowds filled the streets, stopped and stared,
Then screams, and the scent of fear
And the sulphur-filled air. We began to run,
With the crowds and their cries, blind, choking,
Stumbling, and turning to stone.

The darkness continued, our legs were numb
As the rivers ran red, like the fires of hell
And the lava rained down, ash fell like snow,
Stifled, smothered, gasping for air,
Vesuvius spewed, and we died where we fell.

THE DARK SIDE

I'm now going to share some of my other poetry with you. Just as I can mostly see the lighter side of everything; I can also see another side, which stirs my creativity in another form. As an artist, I feel I have to portray this darker side too. Some of you may find the following disturbing.

CROW PEOPLE

At the back of a shop in the centre of town,
They scavenge for cans and bottles.
The old bag lady, her worldly goods stashed
In a shopping trolley, she shares with the pisser.
They share an old couch, along with a few rats.
It's wet and stinks of shit and worse.

Friday night and the white shirts have had their fun.
They stagger and piss, puke and fall on those asleep
In doorways, nursing their bottles and cans.
A few grunts and slurred words,
The shirts move on. Bag lady wrapped in tarpaulin
Snores, curled up on her couch.

Saturday morning, the rain pours down. Slowly like
snails
In a race, they grovel in the trash, dry tab-ends,
Discarded takeaways. Food for the stomach,
Drink for the soul. A match is struck. Raucous
Coughs from the waking-dead, as they stumble
Into another bloody day in Paradise.

NIGHTMARE

The garden is breath-taking; I breathe the air, sweet with the scent of almonds.
Japonica, Jasmine, Sandalwood, Driftwood and sweet-scented pine.
I lay beneath the swaying Palm; wafting arms lull me into sleep.

Dark shadows fill my dreams, the wafting palm replaced by limbs old, gnarled and grey with fingers long and tinged with blood. They move towards my open chest and grab my heart and hold it high above my ribs.

I hear it pump, boom-boom, boom-boom, blood fills my eyes and seeks my nose, my mouth and slithers down my throat, filling my lungs, I'm choking. Help me someone, help me.

Through eyes of red, I scream for help with soundless voice; my lips sealed shut. I am held fast and cannot run; there's no escape – I must I must, my heart still beats, boom-boom, boom-boom.

Then soaked in sweat and fading red, departing grey, my eyes now blink, my lips unsealed, I feel the coarseness in my throat and raging thirst, my heart still beats. The swaying Palm wafts its arms.

SUFFUSION

In the depth of the night
She came and stood by my bed
And reached towards me with an arm of sinewy bone
Her fingers cold and stiff
Her eyes dark hollows.
Tight lips sealed shut.
Mother.
A chill ran over my skin, like mist on a winter's morn
As she passed through me.
I awoke to a new day
And knew who'd killed my father
And who would be next.

ELEVEN SECONDS

For the lone white dove, his life will end –
In eleven seconds.
Grasped by a stealthy predator with uncurled talons -
Scrapyard grab-crane.
With hungry eyes, the hawk sights his prey.
On streamlined wings, dives and grasps.
As a tin opener pierces a can, its razor sharp
Beak rips into the snow white chest.
The dove's heart still beats.
The hawk's wings droop, shrouding its catch.
Feathers broken and bloodied,
One faint cry – the hawk feeds.

BOGEYMAN

Come with me, child, I'll take you away, to the magic land where you can play.
Puddles to splash in of red, green and blue, and purple spotted elephants that live in the trees and slide down the necks of chequered giraffes.

Look into my eyes: see spinning red circles that will take you up high,
Where children have wings and soar through the skies, then swim with the dolphins, down in the depths, see mermaids on coral reefs combing their hair.

Did mummy tell you to turn and flee from the sweet-bearing stranger who'll take you away? You'll not see the magical land with castles on high, where pink-winged unicorns fly in the sky, and coin-spilling waterfalls tumble and flow.

Come; stroke this puppy I have under my coat; his fur is so soft, and he's no one to love, his eyes are blue, isn't he beautiful – he looks just like you. He misses his mummy. Would you like to hold him? Then come over here.

Just one step nearer, that's it nearly there, look in my pocket – there's a special treat for you there, take it and lick it, a striped candy bar. Soon you'll feel sleepy in need of rest; you'll fall into my arms. I'll have finished my quest.

THE KILL

Out of the dark, crept the cat, sleek and black,
He's tracked the scent, fresh blood gels by my feet.
Topaz eyes hold mine. I crouch, unmoving.
His whiskers twitch, shoulders hunched.
He yawns, sour breath, purple tongue licks the air.

An arm's length from my reach, my knife -
Stuck in the dead man's chest. The cat nears,
He doesn't want my kill. I am his.
Our eyes still locked. I grab the knife and blink.
He leaps. Thunder in my chest. A dark red mist.

THE GRAVEYARD SHIFT

The graveyard stands above a worked out pit
Where the long dead caught in the subsidence
Slide slowly into the bottom shafts.

Some were miners in their day, and still are,
Now, blackened by time, they toil no more,
Taking it easy, asleep on the job.

Attributed to Tony Harrison for this idea.

THE UNDERGROUND CLUB

For a century they all lay facing north.
A hundred years on and they face east
The next, face south, then others, west.
Configuration – the sign of the cross.

Four-hundred years and the same plot,
Changes. South to North, West to East
The ground levels. New members join
Layer upon layer – without accretion.

Slowly with the passing of time, they
Crumble, disintegrate, rot. Returning to
Earth, dust to dust. Politely
Allowing others into the club.

THE BURQA

What hides behind your gown of black?
A woman with swollen womb, an unborn child
Perhaps a man with wicked plans evil and vile.
Do you smile and dream of names beneath your veil,
Or grin with thoughts of your next kill?

This shroud of black what does it hold?
The bonds of love and ties of life,
Or grenades and guns and sharpened knives?
Befriended in another's land, food and shelter freely given,
While underneath the bomb is set

Uncover your face, what does it show?
Brown eyes, emptiness, compassion, grief, a smile?
Are you my friend? I cannot know, you're locked away
In your fort of black. When I deliver your child
Will I be repaid with a bullet?

MAGNIFICATION

Have you ever looked at yourself in a 15X Magnification mirror? AAAAAARRRGGGGHHHH! Don't. Ever – Ever, you'll never be the same again.

My doctor recently changed my blood pressure tablets and I noticed a rash developing on my neck and chest. This was followed by itching around my eyes and flaky skin, which I couldn't see too well, even wearing my reading glasses when looking into an ordinary mirror. I sent for one of those blemish-loving, extreme close-up, blackhead spotting, whisker finder, eyebrow tweezing, capillary finding, precision optical quality 15X magnification mirrors.

It was like looking at the surface of the moon. Miniscule blackheads were now extinct volcanoes; a tiny spot, an active volcano. Wrinkles, lines, open pores –all fifteen times larger than life. I had more creases than Nora Batty's stockings, and not just crow's feet, their nests were there too.

Seventy-three years old, I looked more like a hundred and seventy three. I likened myself to a 73 year old house. Not much left in the attic, faulty plumbing, occasional damp patches, creaking floors and doors, irregular thermostat.

After I'd aged ten years in five minutes, I took a 'selfie'. Because if I didn't, by the time I got an appointment with the doctor, I would have aged another ten years, and the rash and flaky skin would have gone.

I can't tell you what happened next, I'm still trying to get an appointment.

TIME

My body is crumbling. I am no longer me –
Something is wrong with my anatomy.
Dying cells struggle to pump blood and air,
My waste disposal unit is showing signs of wear.
Vision once sharp and crystal clear
Now dull and blurred as the end draws near.
Loud music and noises vibrate in my ears
Which have grown twice as big over all the years.
My fine golden tresses that once crowned my head
Now grey and wiry, growing elsewhere instead.
Ligaments and tendons once stretched and taut
Now need support socks, perish the thought.
My bones, frail and brittle like crisp brandy snap
Knees so worn they both need new caps.
My skin far too big like twice-kneaded dough
Stretched and pulled so downward it goes.
My lungs that once let me dance through the night
Now wheeze and grown like a set of bagpipes.
And feet that wore heels of four inch or higher
Now stumble and fall as though walking through fire.
Sheer stockings once covered my shapely slim legs,
Now covered in tights made from elasticated thread.
And my pretty neat calves now all shades of blue

My varicose veins look like patterned tattoos.
And where are my teeth? Another big dread
They're in there someplace vanishing into my head
My head is full of a lifetime's knowledge.
'You're old and don't know things.'
Is how young folk acknowledge.

THE ULTIMATE GIFT

It was nothing that made the headlines at the time, but it's something I've never forgotten and never will. Shortly after 9/11, the Kenyan Masai generously gave fourteen cows to the American people as a gesture of sympathy.

Now, this might not seem much, but to the Masai, their cows are their most valuable possession after their children.

The cows were handed over to William Brancick, deputy head of the US embassy in Kenya. The ceremony was marked by tribespeople in traditional red robes and jewellery, some of whom carried banners saying 'To the people of America, we give these cows to help you.'

Many of the Masai have no running water, electricity or telephones. Details of the tragic events of 9/11 were described to the tribespeople by Kimeli Naiyomah, a Kenyan-born man who was studying in New York at the time.

On his return, his recollection of the events was the first time they had heard of the attacks in New York and Washington which killed more than 3,000 people. Mr Naiyomah described the extensive fires and the sight of people jumping from the tall buildings. Most of his audience didn't know what a skyscraper was.

Think about this unselfish act of the Masai people for a minute and get it into perspective. Compare the differences between the size of the countries and the two peoples and how the Masai, who can be fierce and deadly if provoked, can easily cry for the pain and suffering of others.

This is the ultimate gift a Masai can give, and to present a cow is the highest expression of regard and sympathy.

I enjoy writing poems about statues and often think about what they would say if they could talk.

PERSEUS WITH THE HEAD OF MEDUSA

Come now good people, there is nothing to fear
Medusa the Gorgon – her head I have here.
What's that I hear – one hundred obols?
You mock me, good sir, 'tis drachmas she's worth.

She can no longer harm you; her eyes cannot see,
Her power is gone, her tongue is now stone.
For one thousand drachmas, I'll throw in the sword.
Where are the high bidders – come, raise up your hands?

Just one thousand drachmas and then I'll be gone,
Off to the market for a toga to wear.
Who shouted 'I'll have it'? Come, open your purse
Your counting's correct sir, the trophies are yours.

OLD PIT CHIMNEY

Oy! You...Don't just stand there, that's what I'm doing.
Tall and useless, not worked for fifty years – half my life.
Only Wheely here to talk to, we've long run out of things
to say.
Occasional dog walker passes by.

Either knock me down or fire me up just like the good
old days,
Furnace roaring, wheels spinning, miners digging,
ponies pulling,
Smoke belching, sirens whining, lift shafts clanging
Action, action, lots of action.

Oy! Don't just turn away, I haven't finished talking yet.
How would you like it, standing here in all weathers?
With nothing to do, eh? Think on what I've said?
And if upon your travels, you happen on Fred Dibnah –
Tell him I'd like a word.

THE STATUES OF EASTER ISLAND

A'say Alan, how long 'ave we been standing here?
Don't look at me Wilf, don't look, look straight ahead.
Why can't we look at each other, Alan?
We'll fall over, Wilf, look what happened to Jim.

A'say Alan, is that him laid on the ground, front row?
Yep, and once you're down you never get up.
Joe at the end says we've been here a thousand years.
It'll seem like that to him; he gets all the rain and wind.

A'say Alan, my body's dead stiff with all this standing.
Ah, another few thousand years and you'll get used to it.
We're famous you know, people travel miles just to see us.
Is that why we have to stay still so they can take pictures?

A'say Alan, I'll be glad when they're gone, and we can relax.
Yea, whose turn is it to keep watch tonight, is it Fred's?
Naa, I think its Lofty's. Is it your turn Lofty?
It's always my turn, I don't know why you bother to ask.

A'say Alan, Sid says we were Meerkats once –
In a past life, do you think it could be true?
Listen, Wilf, I've told you before, don't take any notice
O' what Sid says. Why do you think he wears that daft
hat?

HOUSE FOR SALE

'It's small and compact,' the agent said. 'Ideal for the
first-time buyer.
Detached, rural, elevated position with scenic views
Southerly aspect. Just needs a little TLC.
Seller will negotiate on price.'
I'll bet he will, I thought.
I looked at him
and his rose-coloured specs
And back at the tumble-down shack.
Blinked, rubbed my eyes and blinked again.
He stepped forward –'Like to see inside?'
He said, as he turned.
But I had gone.

WAITING FOR THE BUS

- I feel as if we've been waiting for ages, what time is it?
- Dunno. My watch has gone.
- We never waited this long in the old days, did we?
- No, half an hour at most.

- I'll tell you summat if it doesn't come soon
I'm going home.
Bloomin' freezing sat here, waiting, for what?
A number nine bus.

- If it doesn't come soon my bus pass'll run out.
Ey up! Here it comes,
And look at that, would you believe it?
The's two of 'em.

THE KISS

Wow! That was some snog, Francesca.
Sure was, do you think we've won?
I hope so after all that, how long did it last?
Minutes, hours or centuries, I haven't got a clue.

Would have liked to gone a bit further though.
Cheeky! You men are all the same –
Open mouth means open legs – Yea!
But not for the longest kiss competition.

And why did we have to take our clothes off
Eh? I didn't see it in the rules.
They thought it would add some culture
And a little frivolity.

The judges have all gone home now,
Come Paolo, we might as well go too.
I'm sure we'll qualify for the
Guinness Scroll of Records...

DAVID

Ey up our Dave, that sure was some shot –
Felling the big guy with a gut catapult
He towered above thi, wielding his sword
But tha were unmoving,
Standing thi ground.

Yes mate, My weapon, a sling and a handful
Of stones, only one did I need to hit the right spot
I carefully stalked round him, slingshot in hand,
Biding my time Then fate took a hand
As his sandals slipped
His body unsteady, he stumbled towards me,

185

Now was my chance, my sling at the ready
With one loaded stone, I swung it with purpose
Faster, and faster my arm did spin, my hearing
Distorted with the constant hum.

But my vision was perfect and the spot now
In sight, mid forehead I aimed for and let
Go of the sling and the stone reached its mark
In less time than a blink. His mouth wide open
As he fell to his death

I waited a moment, the crowd became still
As I walked to my conquest and took up his
Sword. His last breath taken,
I looked at my foe and his seven foot length
Then raised up his sword and hacked off his head.

My, that's a great tale Dave, tha's done thi dad
Proud, and all those who saw it said out loud
Not once did you flinch, a hero they said,
They're down at the pub to buy you a beer
...I'd put some kecks on though.

Sir John de Creke, 1325
Westley Waterless, Cambridgeshire

A KNIGHT'S TALE

Which dafter bugger invented this?
Just how am I supposed to piss?
As for doing a number two –
Tell me please, what do I do?

With metal breastplate and heavy chainmail
All to protect from a lance's impale
With all this weight I cannot hurry
And need to swiftly after last night's curry

As for fighting in a bloody war
It's hardly likely with my arse so sore,
I can barely move wearing hammered steel
But so I must to attain the privy seal.

John Bunyan's a lot to answer for
Writing poems about hardiness and valour
'He who would valiant be...'
Just doesn't work, when you're dying to pee

I can hardly see through this 'ere visor
Yet I've received a letter from the King's advisor.
Prepare for battle the message reads
And climb upon thine armoured stead

To fight for one's country is a gallant deed
The king is our leader so I go with God's speed
A fearsome trump I'm holding back
Which could be handy for a counter attack.

QUORA

Have any of you seen Quora on the internet? Apparently it is a place to share knowledge and better understand the world. It is a platform to ask questions and connect with people who contribute unique insights and quality answers. Nothing wrong with that, you might think.

Quora is a site which opens your mind to a vast range of subjects, from physics to art and where you will find answers to impossible questions, such as, which came first – the chicken or the egg? And, what happens when an unstoppable force meets an immovable object? What comes after the universe and space?

Many questions are of the type only people with a mind like the late Professor Stephen Hawking could answer. Yet some of the questions are the extreme opposite as you will see shortly. These are the questions that take my interest. Bearing in mind, the Quora moderation team expect all answers to be complete, precise, satisfying and somewhat lengthy, and most of them are. Accurate and informative answers are given from masters of their particular fields. And I am thankful, having sometimes been in need of answers myself, for the time these experts take to reply to such a wide variety of questions.

Because this book is a light-hearted look at life and language, and most probably because I spent many years in the 'Funny Business', I enjoy reading the type of questions you don't expect to find on Quora. And because I hate long lengthy answers (politicians take note) I see opportunities for me to give my answers, which are all based on the KISS system, which I may have mentioned before. Keep It Simple, Stupid.

Here are a few of the questions and my own answers.

Q: Is the world going to end on 18/4/18?
A: As it is now the 20th of April, I think it's highly unlikely.

Q: Do you prefer the right or left side of the bed?
A: The one nearest the toilet.

Q: What would you call pants where the crotch comes down almost to the feet?
A: Ballocks.

Q: If you were about to be executed by firing squad, what one last thing would you ask for?

A: A suit of armour.

Q: If you walk into a room full of people and everyone stops and looks at you, what would you say?

A: If male: 'Is this the waiting room for the sperm bank?'

If female: 'Are you all together?'

Q: If someone had a gun to your head and said 'Tell me a fast fact or die', what would you say?

A: 'I removed the bullets.'

Q: If you were a light bulb what type would you be?

A: The brightest.

Q: You awake one morning and find you have changed into a cat. What would you do?

A: Look for the litter tray.

Q: I loaded my magazine wrong in my LC380 and now a bullet is jammed in the chamber facing the wrong way. What should I do?

A: Are you sure you should be handling a firearm?

Q: Why do stars look so small? Give a one word answer.

A: Space.

Q: If a person suddenly stops smoking, what will happen to him?

A: The fire will have completely gone out and nothing left but ash. Oh! Did you mean he'd stopped smoking cigarettes? I'll leave that answer for the experts.

Q: What would happen if someone with an army decided to invade South America?

A: They'd look around and decide someone had beaten them to it.

Q: What would the world be like without pencils?

A: Pencilless.

Q: What would the world be like if cars didn't exist?

A: We would be knee-deep in horse muck.

Q: What would the world be like without the light?

A: Dark.

Q: Where would I be if I never existed?

A: A glint in your father's eye.

Q: You wake up on an autopsy table. What do you do?

A: Ask for a blanket.

Q: What would your last words be if you knew you only had 7,000.000 seconds to live?

A: Is that clock right?

Q: Your daughter is kidnapped, and the criminals demand a ransom you cannot possibly pay. If you contact the police, they will kill her. What do you do?

A: Send for Liam Neeson.

Q: How do you write a blank verse poem?

A: Here's one I wrote earlier...

Q: What would you do if a bear broke into your house at midnight and you had no gun?

A: Sit him down at the table, give him a bowl of porridge and tell him my name is Goldilocks.

Q: Is it possible for you to respond to this question without using the letter A?

A: Yes.

These are genuine questions and answers taken from my Quora.

TRIVIA TIME

Here are a few more bits of trivia for you.

In 1997, 39 people in Britain attended hospital with, you're not going to believe this – tea-cosy-related injuries!
How the hell can you get injured with a tea cosy?

A *corpocracy* is a society ruled by corporations and a *coprocracy* is one ruled by shits.

The French mathematician Descartes believed that monkeys and apes could talk but kept quiet in case they were asked to work.
No comment!

England lost to Argentina during the World Cup on the 30th of June 1998 on a penalty shoot-out. On that day and the following few days, the number of heart attacks in England increased by 25%.
It's only a game!

Eh, this is scary. Established writers and artists are 18 times more likely to kill themselves than the general population.

So, if I don't finish this book, you know the reason, and if you don't finish the book – it could be you.

THE TIMES THEY ARE A-CHANGIN'

Have you ever noticed how times are changing? Not always for the better, eh? I could give so many instances it would fill a book, now there's a thought!

The incident I'm going to tell you about occurred around 1967/68. It was one Boxing Day and we had gone to meet some friends in their local pub. They didn't have a car so had walked. It was around noon when we pulled into the car park, which was near the Sheffield Wednesday football ground and entered the pub.

Just over three hours later when we were leaving, we found that our car was at the very back of the car park and was now blocked in by the football supporters' cars.

We walked along the road where more cars were parked until we found another Mini. My hubby placed our car key in the lock and it opened. The four of us entered and we drove to our friends' house about a mile away and stayed there for a couple of hours.

At five o'clock, we drove back to the pub and most of the cars had gone. There was just one chap standing in the car park, leaning against our Mini. We pulled alongside and got out of his car. John explained the situation.

The chap smiled.

'I reckoned that must have been what happened,' he said as we got into our respective cars. 'I knew you'd be back – your car is in better nick than mine.' He grinned and nodded towards our Mini, smiled again and waved as he drove away.

Oh Happy Days.

POETRY SHOWCASE

I've now got some very special poetry for you to read, written by some poets who are published and some who write for the love of it, and whom I'm privileged to know.

JOURNEY

The first man who sat next to me was a bear,
thick fur, sour breath, paws like ski gloves.
Said he was having a tough ride at work.
Fleas played hopscotch on the back of his neck.
I pressed close to the window, saw my own reflection,
the world playing across it like a cine film.
When he got off, he left a crumpled newspaper on the seat
and the smell of his worries, like overripe fruit.

The second man was a cockerel, made his foot
into a fist to shield his cough. Bits of grit
came out with his breath, sounded like lead shot
on the carriage floor. He pulled a laptop from under
his wing, logged on, Googled the words 'Thai Brides'.
A hundred thumbnail photos appeared.
Now and then he clicked on a picture, peered
so close his beak tapped the screen.

The third man to take the seat was a pig, got on
at Derby, pink-skinned, bloated, vest-top two sizes
too small, blond hair on his forearms almost
long enough to comb. He smelt of Lynx,
stashed a carrier bag full of lager under the seat,
rested his shank against mine. Coming into Sheffield,
the lights shivered, dipped. Static between his shell suit
trousers and my nylon tights made fireflies in the dark.

Julie Mellor

This poem won the Yorkshire prize in the York Open
Poetry Competition.

MY MEMORY

Your gleaming coat of feathery greys
is mine alone and mine to stroke.
I hold you still and feel the warmth,
your small, soft body against my cheek,
contented murmurs, yours and mine.
We shared a time. You, mine alone
when tiny paws trod at my lap.
Sweet mischief, just a memory now,
you never grew from kittenhood.
You had to learn but never did.
That road divides us ever more.
I miss soft fur, those tiny paws
that paddled gently at my cheek.
That soft, grey body, warm to stroke
Stays kitten-like in memory.

Jeannette Ayton

INTEGRITY

I am a British MP honest and true
The colour of my party is bright bright blue
And hand on heart I never will
Accidently put my fingers in the tax payers' till

I am a government minister and the people I have led
Are members of the party that is deep deep red
And honestly I say that I never will
Accidently put my fingers in the tax payers' till

I am a liberal gentleman, a right good fellow
And the colour of my party is a bright sunny yellow
So I'll say to you that I never will
Accidently put my money in the tax payers' till

We are the jolly members of the parties three
And we all are as honest as only we can be
So we'll all sing together this bright refrain
That we promise to be good till we can cheat again.

Glenda Griffiths

DIRECTION

My bees are dancing bees.
They dance in a circle
Then figure of eight,
With a waggle of the body
That reaches to the sun.

My bees will dance to flowers
That lie in the four corners of the wind.
I practise their dance
And my hum fills the summer.

My bees are stinging bees
That tear themselves open
In the dance of death.

Marion New

DAWN CHORUS

Dawn chorus – birds wake up and sing
As each spring morning's light
Comes creeping soft.

Not in our house. Unwittingly we host
A daily Morris workshop – North-west-Clog –
It's our own ceilidh, right here in our loft.

Ah, feathered choristers, folks used to say –
We've got a feathered bloomin' Glastonb'ry,
Where everybody's danced the night away!

The jackdaws in the chimney stamp and swear,
Trying to find their tents and put their boots on,
Dear oh dear!
They've clearly had a right old time of it –
Their loud remarks and chortles make us jump,
Coffee goes everywhere.

Starlings – get this, mate! They can do each
Ringtone that they pick up in the street,
Clattering milkman, whistling gardener,
Muzac that bounces from each open car –
A pop of corks, a giggling, wheezing toke –
The Lord knows what they smoke.

Sparrows beneath the eaves
Squat empty swallows' nests –
Just till they're back off holiday, you know,
Good neighbours that they are –
Talk in stage whispers, endless, restlessly,
Peek in our window, just to see what's what,
And click their nervous toes
As daylight grows.

Dawn chorus in our cottage,
In the peaceful countryside –
I want to pull the duvet up
And hide.

Liz Parkhurst

UNDER THE APPLE TREE

I would like to be that woman sitting under the apple
tree
In her comfortable wicker chair
A book lies open on her lap
Under her folded hands.

You could be forgiven for thinking she were asleep
See, she tilts her head
As she watches the younger children skipping.
They are singing a song from her childhood

'Mother in the kitchen – doing a bit o' stitching'
The woman claps her hands
The children turn smiling faces to her
And carry on with their skipping rhyme

I wish I were that woman sitting under the apple tree
The picnic hamper lies on the tartan rug
Filled with delicious fayre
Waiting for the eager children

She is, I should imagine, the grandmother,
Dressed in a long skirt and wearing a purple blouse
A large-brimmed straw hat
Shields her from the scorching sun

There is a stillness about her,
When she speaks it is in a genteel tone:
She picks up the open book
And calls the children to finish their game

I wish I were that woman sitting under the apple tree
I watch as she softly reads
The children sit on the blanket

Their heads resting on her lap
Listening.

Maureen Ryan

CAPTURING TIME

If I could hold moments in my hand
Remember the tangy smell that filled my nostrils
The ripe redness of Worcester Pearmains
The yellow-green shining of James Grieves
Feel the bucket hefted on my shoulder
The stretch of muscles as I reached high
With sunlight filtering through the leaves
Hear the buzz of bees feasting on overripe fruit
Would it take me to that carefree summer?
As a student when life was still packed
Like apples on newspaper waiting for maturity.

Rae Moyise

DELAYS POSSIBLE UNTIL 2017
(Motorway Warning Sign)

It was pleasant enough at first.
2016. June. Warm sun. Slight breeze.
After the first hour many took to sunbathing
on the grassed motorway bank
among the purple lupins.
I watched a Kestrel quivering against blinding blue
watching me
watching him.
After all, what could we do but wait
outside time as we were,
and eat stale crisps from each other's' glove
compartments.

By July I'd worked up quite a friendship
with the woman from the Rover in front
exchanged the tales behind our scars
while her husband sulked under the bonnet.

August.
Sun-tan well-developed. Motorway
Surveillance helicopter still
Dropping sandwiches and beer at irregular intervals.

September brought new bursts of celebration from the
kids
who wouldn't be going back to school yet awhile.
Complaints began about sandwich fillings
and the fact that people were taking less care to relieve
themselves away from the home bank.
I found I could sleep for a week at a time.

By October/November, hibernation was setting in.
More people slept, car seats tilted well back,

209

for longer and longer.
(The helicopter had dropped blankets.)

By Christmas, cheer was notably absent
Even though a small cracker was knotted
to each turkey sandwich pack
with tinsel.
The couple in the Rover had locked their doors
and stopped answering shouted enquiries about their
well-being.
Certainly their car never rocked rhythmically now.
We wondered at the complete absence
of misty net curtains
of condensation.

New Year. No-one emerged
as Champagne bottles smashed on the tarmac,
their little silver celebratory parachutes
having proved too frail
to sustain hope.

Ann Hamblen

CELEBRATION ON THE HIGH ARCH

During the hours of darkness I come alive.
Scent-driven, satnav-guided,
free running the urban fox trail,
the discarded trolley highway
through ginnels, litter and railing gaps

to the girdered arches
rising above the gorge
and the channel's puckered flesh.
Here, I dream my full height.

Above the traffic roar,
random firefly lights,
above the box-ticked life,
on tip-toe I crest the wind.

Here I do not ask what if?
I suck in my senses,
ignore the threat from the east and
balance everything.

Look at me, Ma,
I am Jimmy Cagney, Nelson,
a building top Gormley,
Cristo Redentor.

Here, risen from the earth,
braving the blast,
and forged in flames,
I run pure and true
like water.

Published in 'Listening to Owls,' by John Irving Clarke

FISH FINGERS

One thing that puzzles and teases and lingers.
Is if a fish has no hands how come it's got fingers?
One thing I need to know to set me at ease.
Is why I've never heard an Eskimo sneeze?

Another thing that's constantly baffling me,
Is if a fly gets scared – does it turn round and flea?
A problem that makes my mind feel like it's shrunk,
Is does an elephant pack all it clothes in one trunk?

And if owls only wake when it's time for the night,
How do they know if they like the day light?
And where is the mouth to be found on a worm?
Is a puzzle that makes my brain wriggle and squirm.

If a bird can fly then why can't a fly bird?
Is a question which may sound strangely absurd?
If a bat is so blind then how can it see cricket balls?
And if water can't climb how can it waterfall?

If eggs came before chickens then who built the nest?
Always puts my poor mind to the ultimate test.
If a dog has a flea does a flea have a dog?
Makes the' wheels of my brain turn like a cog.

If ice cream is cold why is it kept in the freezer?
Is certainly a difficult crazy brainy teaser.
If a pig could go 'moo' would it just be a cow?
I think that it could – but I don't see how?

And if the river in Paris is called the Seine,
If you ever fall in it – are you insane?
The answers to these questions I just can't see,
So if you know them – can you tell me?

Sally Kate Taylor

LAMENT FOR AN ENDANGERED SPECIES

O perfect pangolin,
trundling armour plating along the tangled forest floor,
precise scales pearly as oyster shells,
pinging like chain-mail,
pauvre petit pangolin,
his days are numbered,
life's challenging, galling.

The poacher's out to skin him, fling him
on his back in the dangling sack.
Shiny blades swingeing, he'll wrangle him, flense him,
so hide away, pangolin, your funeral bell's clanging,
the mandolin's plangent dirge
twanging, jingle-jangling.

Pathetic guileless pangolin,
no time to dilly-dally,
curling's no protection,
the ball's set rolling,
best get going,
your situation's no-win,
a no-where-man is pangolin.

Sue Riley

THE GIRL FROM IPANEMA

She was the girl from Ipanema walking barefoot in the sand
In her designer topless swimsuit, oh so beautifully tanned.

She would dance to the bossa nova, under dreamy starry skies,
Now she's had a hip replacement and cataracts on her eyes.

She posed for the photographers, drinking Daiquiri with rum,
And now had a colonoscopy with a camera up her bum.

Time goes by, the years just fly and life keeps getting harder,
So now she drinks Sanatogen and not Pina Colada.

She had her nights of passion in the villa by the sea,
Now when she gets up four times a night, it's just to have a pee.

The girl from Ipanema has now become an O.A.P.
Instead of Cuba Libras all she drinks is cups of tea.

Joyce Watling

THE LITTLE THINGS

Just a ray of sunlight, in the month of May,
A smile to come home to after a long and stressful day.
A full cup of coffee that I can balance on my knee,
Looking at old photos, thinking, gosh that must be me!
The first fall of snow that covers the entire town,
The last dark night, when summer comes around.
Driving in the darkness and seeing a sky full of stars,
A friend that makes the effort to send a birthday card.
'Good morning' from a stranger whom I've never seen before,
Picking up sea shells that have been washed upon the shore.
Walking through the country with my loved ones close behind,
They're just the little things that come into my mind.

Katie Donoghue

HIS FACE LOOKED FAMILIAR

But I didn't know why,
Then a vague distant memory made me feel rather shy.
The man I remembered was young and strong,
Was it his father? Why had he sat there so long?
Who are you? I asked, his face just a void.
Why won't you answer? I was feeling annoyed.
The stranger just sat there and silently stared
I began to feel anxious, worried and scared.
Where is my love? I asked. Where has he gone?
My darling, my love, I have been here all along.
His face looked familiar but I didn't know why.

Michelle Cleary

Thank you poets for letting me share. There's some talented people out there.

Before we move on, there are two poems that when I first saw them, have stuck in my mind since. In my mother's later years, she had Alzheimer's and eventually had to go into a care home. We had done all we could, but she was becoming a danger to herself and us. There's more about my Mum and this illness in the third book in my trilogy.

We were waiting to see the manageress and the following two poems were framed on the office wall. No one knows who wrote them, but I think they are equally touching and memorable and deserve a place in this book.

CRABBY OLD WOMAN

What do you see, nurses, what do you see?
What are you thinking when you're looking at me?
A crabby old woman who's not very wise,
Uncertain of habit, with faraway eyes?

Who dribbles her food and makes no reply.
When you say in a loud voice, 'I do wish you'd try!'
Who seems not to notice the things that you do
And forever is losing a stocking or shoe?

Who, resisting or not, lets you do as you will,
With bathing and feeding, the long day to fill?
Is that what you're thinking? Is that what you see?
Then open your eyes, nurse, you're not looking at me.

I'll tell you who I am as I sit here so still,
As I do at your bidding, as I eat at your will.
I'm a small child of ten with a father and mother,
Brothers and sisters who love one another.

A young girl of sixteen with wings on her feet
Dreaming that soon now a lover she'll meet.
A bride soon at twenty my heart gives a leap,
Remembering the vows that I promised to keep.

At twenty-five now, I have young of my own,
Who need me to guide, and a secure happy home.
A woman of thirty, my young now grown fast,
Bound to each other with ties that should last.

At forty, my young sons have grown and are gone,
But my man's beside me to see I don't mourn
At fifty once more, once more children play round my
knees,

219

Again we know children, my loved one and me.

Dark days are upon me, my husband is dead,
I look at the future, I shudder with dread.
For my young are all rearing young of their own,
And I think of the years and the love that I've known.

I'm now an old woman and nature is cruel
Tis jest to make old age look like a fool.
The body, it crumbles, grace and vigour depart,
There is now a stone where I once had a heart.

But inside this old carcass a young girl still dwells,
And now and again, my battered heart swells.
I remember the joys, I remember the pain,
And I'm loving and living life over again.

I think of the years all too few, gone too fast,
And accept the stark fact that nothing can last.
So open your eyes, nurse, open and see
Not a crabby old woman...Look closer – see ME

A NURSE'S REPLY

To the 'Crabby Old Woman'

What do we see, you ask, what do we see? Yes, we are thinking when looking at thee!

We may seem to be hard when we hurry and fuss, but there's many of you, and too few of us.

We would like far more time to sit by you and talk, to bath you and feed you and help you to walk.

To hear of your lives and the things you have done; your childhood, your husband, your daughter, your son.

But time is against us, there's too much to do – patients too many, and nurses too few.

We grieve when we see you so sad and alone, with nobody near you, no friends of your own.

We feel all your pain, and know of your fear
That nobody cares now your end is so near.

But nurses are people with feelings as well, And when we're together you'll often hear tell

Of the dearest old Gran in the very end bed, And the lovely old Dad, and the things that he said,

We speak with compassion and love, and feel sad when we think of your lives and the joy that you've had,

When the time has arrived for you to depart, you leave us behind with an ache in our heart.

When you sleep the long sleep, no more worry or care,
there are other old people, and we must be there.

So please understand if we hurry and fuss –
There are many of you, And so few of us.

They always bring a tear to my eye.

STRANGE CUSTOMS

There's another holiday resort I've been to that had strange customs. I suppose I should say they were different to ours, but perhaps we had similar customs a century or so ago.

We were on in Morocco in a place called Agadir, a city on Morocco's southern Atlantic coast, in the foothills of the Anti-Atlas Mountains. A smart looking place with 4 and 5-star hotels, clean, fresh and modern in true Arabic style, very different to some areas of Morocco we had been to. And then I learned that it had been rebuilt after an earthquake in 1960, although some of the old walls remain.

Agadir was no different to other areas of Morocco regarding customs and culture. They were obviously trying to attract tourists and were succeeding in a far different way to what you would find in Spain, France, Portugal and Italy.

Extremely friendly people, always chatting to the Brits, not all of them spat at you if you didn't buy their taqiyah and fez hats, trinkets, carpets, brass kettles and hookahs.

Some were quite pleasant with a good knowledge of the English language and would come and sit and chat with you asking questions about life in England.

Some had relatives in Manchester and London, and would ask if you would kindly take a sealed parcel containing a leather jacket back with you and post it on when you returned home as postage was too expensive from Morocco!

You could always keep in touch with them when you were back home as well, by swapping names and addresses, so they could write and tell you of their education and how they were progressing with their knowledge of English because of your help. You might even see them again – six weeks later they could be standing on your doorstep with a box of oranges, looking for a place to stay.

We walked down to the fishing harbour one day. The smell of rotting fish and sewage undertones in forty degree heat still sticks in my throat; this was nothing like Whitby.

The noise was deafening, with hundreds of small wooden boats, blue in colour, jostling for space on the dirty water. Crates of fish being hauled onto the quayside, angry bartering over prices, dirhams changing hands as the purchasers placed the unwrapped fish in the hoods of their djellabas.

Older men with sun-baked skin, sat with questionable cigarettes dangling from their lips as they repaired nets and plastic carrier bags.

Craftsmen carved timber for new boats, while beggars and fish-restaurant owners pestered tourists.

I wanted to leave this sprawling mayhem. Give me the Spanish gypsies any day, I said as we made our way to the souk.

The souk market still had sewage undertones but thankfully lacked the rotting fish smell. Here was another area of diversity. Thirsty and exhausted donkeys stood without cover in the baking sun. Camels groaned as yet another pair of tourists was loaded onto their backs.

Males, young and old, squatted on cushions, drinking mint tea and smoking from hookahs. Water-sellers constantly ringing their bells and wearing colourful garments and large tasselled hats, poured drinking water from sheep or goats bladder containers, complete with the animals leg and foot, into small brass cups hung on leather belts across their chests.

Fire eaters, fire walkers, acrobats and snake-charmers provided entertainment. Colourful stalls were spread around the square with over-keen merchants desperate for sales.

Crowds of locals handled bizarre, dangerous and probably illegal items, all displayed on bright-coloured cloths. Knives, machetes, powdered horn and roots from protected species, tobacco, used spectacles and false teeth, that passed from mouth to mouth until the purchaser found the most comfortable fit, placing the used ones unwashed back on the counter, with a following argument as to why they should cost more because the set contained a gold tooth.

The day drew to a close and we made our way to the steps along the beach where we sat to watch the sunset. The Muezzin began his long mournful wail calling the people to prayer. A youth walking along the beach, turned when he saw us. Oh no I thought, not another one.

'Hello,' he said, smiling as he came towards us and held out his hand. 'My name is Ammar.'

Not wanting to be too unsociable, we said hello and shook hands. We told him a different hotel when he asked where we were staying. He sat down with us and looked at John's Nike trainers and said how much he liked them and would John give them to him. We said no and left. Eventually, after a few more days of Ammar asking for the shoes, John said he could have them on the night before we left.

Every time we saw Ammar in the days that followed, he always said how much he was looking forward to the shoes – he didn't care that they would be far too big.

On the evening before we left, after packing, we kept our promise and met Ammar on the steps by the beach. He was carrying a rolled-up carpet over his shoulder. John handed him a carrier bag containing his two-week-old trainers. Ammar put down the carpet and smiled as he removed his precious gift. Taking off his sandals, he slipped his feet into the trainers and placed the old sandals in the carrier.

'Thank you John, thank you Jackie, I am grateful to your kindness, thank you, thank you.' He couldn't stop shaking our hands. The look on his face was like a child's on Christmas morning. He suddenly let go of our hands.

'I must go and show my friends, thank you.' He backed away from us, still holding out his hands, then turned and ran down the steps and onto the beach.

'Ammar,' we shouted. 'You've forgotten your carpet.'

He stopped and turned. 'No, that is my gift for you for the shoes, thank you.' He turned again and continued along the beach.

ROBERT

Another interesting character we met was a chap called Robert. As we were in Morocco and he was big and black with afro hair, we assumed he had taken on the name purposely. Impressing the tourists was paramount; why else hang around in hotel lobbies? But there was something different about this man. The hotel doormen covered the doors 24 hours a day and made sure no non-bona fide people entered. So why was this man standing at the bar wearing a smart suit and tie, and talking to the bar staff?

He came towards us as we came down the wide staircase. There was no way we could tell this person that we weren't staying in this hotel.

'Good evening,' he said, in better English than mine. 'Allow me to introduce myself.' He told us his name and led us to the bar. 'Care for a pre-dinner drink?'

'No thanks,' we replied, trying to make our way to the restaurant. 'We're going straight for dinner.' I smiled and carried on walking.

'Never mind, some other time perhaps,' he said and walked back towards the bar. His speech, dress and manner were immaculate. He was our talking point over dinner that evening.

We saw him again the following evening in the foyer; he was talking to another English couple. Politely acknowledging us, he carried on talking. He didn't appear in the bar the following evening nor the next, but as we left the restaurant after dinner we sat by the bar and ordered our drinks.

As soon as the waiter placed them on the counter, Robert appeared and said something in Arabic to the barman. John had already pulled some dinars from his pocket to pay, but the waiter told us that Robert had put the drinks on his account. We now had no option other to talk to him.

'Allow me to introduce myself again, by the way, not a very good landing today, was it?' he said in perfect prose, immaculate white teeth reflecting the light as much as the glass he was holding. He was looking at my hubby, John.

John just stared. 'Oh! The parasailing,' John replied.

'I was at the beach bar and could see there was no way you were going to land on the beach. Were you injured in any way?'

I could laugh about it now but I didn't think it funny at the time, as I saw John's face as he was trying hard to steer the ropes towards the beach. He landed in a hotel garden.

'Luckily I was okay, but the hotel guests weren't too pleased as they deserted their sun-beds and took flight. The guy running the parasailing wasn't too pleased either, when he saw his parachute tangled up in the shrubbery.'

We all laughed and told him our names. I asked him what he was doing in Morocco.

'I sell and repair cars, English cars, Fords.' He wore a signet ring on the fourth finger of his right hand engraved with the initials RWS; his cufflinks matched.

John and I exchanged glances, I was curious. Before I could ask him another question, he asked where in England we came from, and then added –

'No, let me guess, Yorkshire?'

'Sheffield.' I said, surprised.

'I thought so,' he replied, then offered us a Consulate cigarette from what looked like a gold case. 'Do you mind?' he replied when we refused.

We shook our heads as he lit the cigarette with a slim gold lighter. He inhaled and blew the smoke in the opposite direction.

'I know Sheffield well,' he continued.

I looked at John and raised my eyebrows. This is surreal, I thought, the biggest con ever.

'Which team do you support, Sheffield Wednesday or Sheffield United? Drink up, it's not every day I meet someone from my home town.' He nodded to the barman for more drinks.

I was going to say, no thanks, but thought, I'll go along with this, this is hilarious. John proffered to pay for the drinks but the barman refused to take the money.

'Which area of Sheffield we came from?' he asked.

'Owlerton,' I replied, knowing he wouldn't know of this area.'

'Near Hillsborough and the football ground, I know it well, are you from there too, John?'

'No, I'm from Shirecliffe.'

'Well, well, it's a small world isn't it?' he laughed. I lived there too.

'Never!'

'Yes, and when I lived there, I used to go to watch the football at Hillsborough and when I lived in the city, I used to go to...' he hesitated. 'Sheffield United's ground, I think it's called Bramall Lane, is that right John?'

John, shocked, nodded. They got talking about football and the fact that Robert knew Kevin Keegan and some Manchester United players. Where's he getting all this from, I thought. I wanted to believe him but couldn't, and yet he knew the place names.

'What on earth were you doing in Sheffield?' I asked.

He took another drag on his cigarette.

'College, Shirecliffe College and then Sheffield University. Lived in a flat on Hanover Street. Look, you finish your drinks, I have to go.' He stubbed the cigarette in the large glass ash tray, which was immediately removed by the barman and replaced with a clean one.

'I have a nightclub in town and I'm the star turn.' He laughed again. What a happy chap, I thought, but none of this could be true. 'I'll take you there one evening, and if you haven't had enough of belly-dancers, John...' He patted John on the shoulder. 'You've not seen what my club has to offer.'

The doorman opened the door for him as he left, ran down the steps as if he owned the world and stepped into a Ford Capri.

We did see more of Robert. He came to the hotel the following evening with a woven straw folder containing photographs of him during his time in Sheffield. Some photographs showed him standing with other students, with Shirecliffe College and Sheffield University in the background.

Other photographs, taken with other students, were in other areas of Sheffield that John and I knew well. There was a photograph of him receiving his degree with cap and gown bearing Sheffield University's colours. There were more than three with Kevin Kegan, arms on each other's shoulders, and other footballers, and many landmarks of England. The more photos we looked at, the more believable it became.

'I knew you didn't believe me, so I thought I'd bring proof,' he laughed. 'Now are you going to accompany me to my nightclub and watch the show?'

CLIMBING GOATS

Before we leave Morocco, I must tell you about the tree-climbing goats – yes, tree climbing goats. And you'll not just see one goat; you'll see a group of them balancing like acrobats on the thin branches.

Food on the ground for these animals is so sparse that they have taken to climbing trees. They only eat from one type of tree, and that's the Argan tree.

When they have gobbled all the fruit from the lower branches, they climb higher and can reach an impressive 8-10 metres. By performing this spectacular feat, they are helping to produce more Argan trees. Sometime later as they digest the fruit, they will spit out the seeds, and some will pass through their systems.

These 'seeds' are Argan nuts, which are gathered and pressed to make Argan oil, a valuable export to more prosperous countries where it is used in the production of cosmetics and foods.

LAUGHS A GAS

I recently had another investigation at the hospital. Having had similar procedures before, I wasn't looking forward to it. The magnitude of the CAT scanner, with its gaping orifice, purred, concealing its potential.

I was draped in a green hospital gown, which you'd think was a tent, and must be designed for all patients weighing between six and thirty-six stones to be covered in a dignified manner at all times.

A pair of long navy-blue paper shorts with a cute back slit completed my ensemble.

I scrambled onto the narrow bed and immediately got cramp. The radiographer, Claire, and the two nurses, who looked like they should be playing with Barbie Dolls, not investigating back passages, smiled.

I was asked a few questions while the wired cannula was inserted into the crook of my arm. The cannula was firmly fixed and attached to the container of liquid that would shortly fill my veins with a dye that would make me feel hot and as if I'd peed myself. I was asked to turn on my left side.

'Just a little lubricant, Jackie,' said Claire and inserted the gas tube into my waste disposal.

One of the two nurses placed a hand on my shoulder, looked down at me and smiled. 'Comfortable?'

There's no answer to that.

'I'm just going to introduce the gas, Jackie. It will feel uncomfortable but let me know if you have any pain.' More smiles – anyone would think they were attending a wedding.

'I'll yell,' I said. 'Last time it was awful, I was in agony for days after.' With a sharp intake of breath, I was hoping one of them would say *Aw! Poor you, in that case, you'd better get dressed and go home, and not have these nasty examinations.*

But they didn't.

'Turn onto your tummy please, Jackie. I know it's difficult with all these tubes and connectors.'

You're not kidding. I felt my insides expanding as I attempted the near-impossible turn.

'Just a little more gas, Jackie, it's carbon dioxide this time, much better than air.'

'Huh!'

'Now turn onto your other side and then onto your back, that should give the bowel a good coating.'

Caught up in the tent and massive knickers, I rolled over and on to my back, cannula and tube caught in my arm, my tummy bloated. *Help! I'm going to explode.*

'First scan coming up, Jackie. We're going to leave you for a few minutes.'

'WHAT! What do you mean you're going to leave me?'

'We can't be exposed to too much radiation, so we'll be behind the screen.'

I lay unmoving as the new gas inflated my ailing intestines. The bed jerked and began to move towards the mouth of Jaws, then stopped. *I'm all alone, what if the lights fuse, and the power goes off and I'm fastened to this contraption?* I could hear clicking and whirring; the bed jerked and moved again.

...Into the valley of death... half a league, half a league...

The fluid from the cannula filled my veins and body. I was getting hotter.

Cannon to the right of me, cannon to the left...

I glanced around; I had to get out of here. I tried to move my arm, but it was straight back above my head. A voice filled my ears.

'Calm down, Jackie, it's just the cannula fluid entering your bloodstream. Keep your arms straight – and relax.'

The bed jerked and moved again. Be calm, be calm, it's almost over. I closed my eyes. The clicking and whirring stopped and the bed reversed as the nurses appeared.

'That's it, Jackie, all over.'

The fear had gone. I began to laugh as I was dismantled from the apparatus.

'We told you it wasn't too bad,' said Claire. 'But I can't recollect anyone laughing before.'

'I began thinking about what would happen if you were to use Helium gas.'

MAUREEN

I'm going to finish nearer to home, in Yorkshire. Before I do, let me introduce you to Maureen Ryan. Maureen came from York five years ago and lives nearby and is a very dear friend; she is also my mentor and always gives praise to my efforts.

With crippling arthritis, COPD and other ailments, she continuously strives to help others. Maureen is a well-educated lady from York and during her career, has held many prestigious positions. With many accolades to her credit and superior level of intelligence, I have to wonder, why, on the times she accompanies me on my talks, she will always find the strangest of places to sit.

I have seen her sit beneath signs that state: 'DON'T LET THIS HAPPEN TO YOU!' And 'NOT ALL ILLNESSES

ARE VISIBLE'. 'EARLY WARNING SIGNS – SEE BELOW'. Not to mention the everyday signs of HAZARD, CAUTION, BEWARE.

Thanks, Maureen, for always singing my song.

MEANWHILE, IN YORKSHIRE

As much as I love travelling, and accepting what each country, with all its diversities throws at me, there's no place quite like home, and when I see the sheep wearing flat caps and smoking cigarettes, mind you they have cut down, I know I'm back in Yorkshire.

Apart from its much loved beautiful scenery, it considers its food and drinks reputation as the best in Britain. It also boasts more Michelin-starred restaurants than anywhere else in the country (apart from the clogged streets of London and who wants to go there?)

It must be the best, why else are so many films and television productions filmed here? Do you know that over 73 films have been set in Yorkshire? Why? You may ask. Well, Yorkshire folk don't mince words and we call a spade a spade. We are generally warm hearted and welcoming, especially if you know anything about ferret, whippet, and pigeon racing, and are not afraid to be the first to get your hand in your pocket when in the pub.

As you already know, we have our own language in God's own county. You've no doubt heard the Yorkshire War Cry – 'ARRHHH MUCH?' There are enough books already on the Yorkshire dialect and sayings without me adding to them. But I've recently seen a new one doing the rounds and I have no idea who I can attribute this to, but thanks, whoever you are...

Yorkshire Godfatha – *'Okay, which daft bugger's put pigeon 'ead in't bed?'*

Something I've always wondered is why do posh folk (I was going to say Southerners, but I'll not), and television presenters say Baath or Barth instead of Bath? It's the same with Plant, why say Plaant or Plont? And camp, bat, pat; even the simple conjunction 'and', becomes aand or arnd.

When I went to school and was learning to read and write, we were taught to say: 'the cat sat on the mat.' Never once did I hear a teacher say, 'the cart sart on the mart.' These southerners *can* produce sharp 'a's, though. For example, no one has ever pronounced my name as Jarkie or Jarqueline.

Without mentioning Lancashire, where this same issue ensues, there's an argument that's been going on since Sheffield, Rotherham, Doncaster, Barnsley and Penistone, etc., became known as South Yorkshire and Leeds, Bradford, Huddersfield and Wakefield etc., became known as West Yorkshire. This is how things are in Yorkshire, slightly complicated.

SMALL ROUND BREAD CAKES: you may know them as bread rolls, baps, cobs, whatever? Let's get this straight once and for all. The plain ones are called bread-cakes and not tea cakes, and the ones with currants and sultanas in are called tea-cakes and not *currant tea cakes*. Don't let anyone tell you any different.

Jack is a common name in Yorkshire, even if it's not your given name. I had an uncle called Jack, but his real name was Joe. It would have been the same if he'd been christened Eric. I've no idea of how or why this originated. Some people may think we use rude words unnecessarily, for example, 'ejaculate'. You will often hear this said if a man goes to work late, it doesn't mean anyone's being rude.

Whitby is a seaside town and port in North Yorkshire, a fishing town well known for its lobsters and crabs and also famous for its abbey, which is supposed to have been home to Bram Stoker's Dracula character.

I was fourteen years old and under age when I went with my friend Lynn to see the 1958 film version, starring Christopher Lee and Peter Cushing. We passed as sixteen-year olds by wearing Queen Elizabeth

Coronation headscarves and clutching large (empty) purses to our chests. The annoying thing was we had to pay full price, adult rate, instead of half price.

I know you're thinking *hang on, what's this have to do with Whitby?* Hold your horses, I'm getting back to that.

The film was terrifying. We were scared out of our wits and too afraid to go home when it finished. Being together gave us a sense of security and a touch of bravado as we laughed and joked, jumping at each other and mimicking the actors, who, less than an hour before had had us shaking in our seats. Yes, I've cleaned that bit up!

It was when we parted company that it got scary, when we had to turn down different streets, knowing we had to enter a dark entry before finding the safety of home.

My granddad died around the same time we saw the *Dracula* film, and during a scene in the film, Dracula was lying quietly asleep in his coffin. Then loud music filled my ears as the vampire suddenly jumped out.

That image was still very much implanted in my mind, and I was too afraid to look at Granddad as he lay in his coffin in the front room with the curtains drawn.

Now we're going to Whitby. The town is a small fishing port on the North coast of Yorkshire. It's famous for its great fish and chips andWhitby Jet, which is a semi-precious stone used in the manufacture of fine jewellery, extremely popular during the Victorian period.

Captain James Cook lived there. Whitby is also famous for the fact that Bram Stoker found his inspiration to write *Dracula* when he stayed there in 1890.

Every year the town has two Goth weekends, abbreviated to WGW. A WGW is a musical event where thousands of fans gather together to listen to music and scare and be scared. The main events are held in the Spa Pavilion but many pubs and hotels also provide live music acts.

You'll be frowned on and classed as a party-pooper if you don't make an effort to dress devilish and bizarre, although some people don't have to make any effort. As well as Goths, Punks and Steampunks, Emos and Bikers of all ages parade around the town, wearing the wildest and weirdest of costumes.

Wearing garlands of garlic around your neck won't protect you from the monsters of every description darting in and out of the secret passages and alleyways, that at one time were used by smugglers. Brides of Dracula, and daughters of Dracula; age is no barrier, as sixteen-year-olds to eighty-somethings all join in the fun.

And the most outstanding character of all, who almost everyone wants to be, is Count Dracula. With white painted face, fake blood dripping down sides of the mouth, black trousers, white frilled shirt and the count's emblem hung on a red ribbon, and a long black and red lined cape and a flat woollen cap...Only in Yorkshire.

Well, that just about sums it up. I have to get on with the third book in my autobiographical trilogy. I hope you've enjoyed reading my tales. Remember, you're never too old to learn something new. I don't have a single qualification to my name, apart from my driving license, and I was seventy when I began writing after retiring. Four years later, and this is my third published book and I have two more in the pipeline.

So, never say never. If I can – you can.

Before I go, do you remember at the start of this book, I was telling you about how I set up the fancy dress business and the countries we sent the costumes to?

Here's the poem I said I would write before finishing the book.

COSTUMES

Polar Bears for Iceland, Centurions bound for Rome,
Mermaids off to Denmark, complete with silver comb,
Belly Dancers, heading south, going to Dubai,
Grass skirts, across the pond, and on to Hawaii.
Ireland wants some bright green Santas,
Scotland's needs are for Aberdeen Angus
And Pipers clad in tartan, kilts a'swaying,
Marching men with bagpipes playing.

Popes, Archbishops, Nuns and Vicars
Some are backless, to wear with naughty knickers!
Film stars, Pop stars, all who are famous
If your face doesn't fit, then please don't blame us.
Henry the eighth and his six wives,
Teddy Boys and Girls for those who Jive.
French maids, French Tarts, 'Allo, Allo.'
Fur-trimmed Santas: 'Ho-ho-ho!'

Little Bo Peep and a flock of sheep
Chicken costumes going 'cheap'!
Jack and Jill with a galvanized bucket
And Lucy Locket – without her pocket.
Humpty Dumpty, Mother Goose
Look out everyone – There's a Gorilla on the loose.
Dracula, Frankenstein, Michael Myers,
Jason Voorhees, and crazy surgeons with rib-joint pliers.

Kings and Queens in flowing robes,
Charming Princes and ugly toads,
Good guys and bad guys from James Bond,
Fairies and Wizards with magic wands.
Bronco Bill and Billy, the Kid
Snakes alive! There's 'Hissing Sid'.
Morris Dancers with bells on their toes

249

And Lady Godiva with the barest of clothes.

Angels, Devils, nice and nasty clowns
Causing havoc running round town.
The wildest of animals, dinosaurs too,
The strangest of costumes we'll make for you.
Elvis the King, in a jewelled white suit,
The Pied Piper of Hamelin with a golden flute.
Pantomime Characters – 'Oh no there isn't.'
'Oh yes there is.' 'He's behind you, 'Oh no he isn't.'

Two-men horses, camels, and cows,
A mammoth of an elephant to a tiny little mouse.
Prawns and Lobsters come up from the deep
And furry black spiders to give you the creeps
Smart uniforms for Great Britannia,
Zulu warriors off to Zambia,
Our seamstresses are greatly skilled
To ensure your character part is fulfilled.

As the saying goes, it's not over till the fat lady sings...

♪♪ *'Always look on the bright side of life'* ♪♪

If you have enjoyed reading *POEMS, PROSE AND TRIPE*, you will enjoy reading my autobiographical trilogy which reads as a novel, and also as stand-alone books.

Book 1

The Girl with the Emerald Brooch

The Girl with the Emerald Brooch: Growing up: 1954 - 1965

by Jacqueline Creek

Link: http://amzn.eu/iWOizIN

Book 2

The Power of Love

The Power of Love: Discovering Myself. 1965-1981

by Jacqueline Creek

Link: http://amzn.eu/j1u8AHx

Book 3

Head for Business Heart for Love

1981 - Present

Available soon

REVIEWS

★ ★ ★ ★ ★
"A blast from the past"
By Basildon: 4 November 2017
"This book took me right back to my childhood and brought back many memories. It was so well written that it stirred my memories of that time and I can't wait to read the next book."

★ ★ ★ ★ ★
"Brilliant...could not put the book down"
By Amazon Customer: 5 March 2017
"Brilliant. Could not put the book down. Read it in 2 days, such a lovely story and because I know the area Jackie lived as a child I could relate to it, I recommend this book to any one, it's great...just waiting now for Jackie's next book."

★ ★ ★ ★ ★
"Memorable"
By Sue: 25 May 2016
"Love, love, loved it. Couldn't put it down. Cannot wait for the next book."

★ ★ ★ ★ ★
"I really enjoyed her honesty"
By Amazon Customer: 1 December 2016
"I could so relate to Jackie's life in Sheffield during the 50/60's, having been born and bred surrounded by terraced houses and Sheffield steel works. I really enjoyed her honesty: it was both funny and sometimes quite moving. A good read. Looking forward to the next one."

★ ★ ★ ★ ★
"A Compelling Read"
By John Irving Clarke: 7 June 2016
"I picked up this book with a little trepidation as misery memoirs are not my thing and I was a little wary after reading the name of Catherine Cookson in the blurb. Surely I was off my reading patch! Not so, as it turns out, this was definitely not the case.

I like books with a solid sense of authenticity, books with characters that emerge from the page as warm, human and flawed. The Girl with the Emerald Brooch has all that in spades and I was hooked from the first few pages, desperately rooting for the central character of Jacqueline, a habitual nail-chewer. But nail-chewing is the least of her worries as from an early age she has onerous care duties which blight her education and life chances. Time and time again fate conspires against her and time and time again she bounces back spirited and resilient.

This is a great read with a rich vein of truth running through it as well as a compelling humour. I don't hand out five star reviews easily, but don't take my word for it, find out for yourself."

★ ★ ★ ★ ★
"Fantastic. A must read!!!!!"
By Sarah: 26 April 2016
"I am in my twenties, so never experienced life back then so thought this book was a great insight. One of the best books I have read in a long time. To be able to laugh, cry and be shocked, all from the same book is a testimony to its content. The writer's personality and passion is seen all throughout the book. I cannot wait for the next edition."

254

★ ★ ★ ★ ★
"A very good and accurate book, which I could relate to."
By Mrs K. E. Bradshaw: 1 January 2017
"This book was a very good and accurate book which I could relate to as I lived locally. The chemist the lady worked in – I recall using it as a little girl when we'd been to Doctor Bark's surgery. I recommend this book. It is a good true story and you won't be disappointed."

★ ★ ★ ★ ★
"A gripping read, a page-turner with laughs and tears."
By Sarah Bennett: 15 March 2016
"A wonderful, gripping read. Great insight into being a teenager in the 50s/60s – every chapter leaves you wanting more! I can't put it down! A fascinating read with laughs and tears. Can't wait for the sequel!

★ ★ ★ ★ ★
"Brings back memories"
By Grammar stickler: 10 November 2017
"I was born in Sheffield and even though I am 10 years younger than Jackie, I know many of the places and situations she writes about. A brilliant book which I really enjoyed."

★ ★ ★ ★ ★
"I loved this book"
By C. Morrison on: 6 April 2017
"I loved this book. I lived in Hillsborough at the same time. I knew the places, went to the same schools, knew

some of the people in it, found it fantastic. I cannot wait for the next one."

★ ★ ★ ★ ★
"A thoroughly enjoyable book"
By Amazon Customer: 5 November 2017
"I really enjoyed this book I found that I could relate to Jackie's journey through life in so many ways. I would recommend this book highly to my friends and family."

★ ★ ★ ★ ★
"Five Stars"
By Steve Deighton: 16 November 2017
"A great read and memory jerker as a teenager in the same era."

★ ★ ★ ★ ★
"You will love this book"
By Sandra Penistone: 7 April 2016
"Life in the 50s and 60s in industrial Sheffield is captured in this book. Jackie's account of her home life will have you smiling and in tears all on the same page. This book tells of hardship and love as a child, her teenage years, and as a young woman. If you like a family saga, this is a must. Looking forward to the next book, Jackie."

★ ★ ★ ★ ★
"A gem!"
By Mal Monroe: 4 November 2017
"I loved Jackie's first book, The Girl with the Emerald Brooch, which is full of heart-warming and really interesting family stories. I got the Kindle version and found it hard to put down. You can't help liking Jackie, her family and all the characters in her books. She writes

in such an open and honest way that you feel that you actually know her. I'm also from Sheffield and grew up not too far from where Jackie did, so I recognise a lot of the names and places she mentions. That said, it doesn't really matter if you have never even been to Sheffield, I'm sure you'll enjoy this book. I'm now half way through her second book and finding that hard to put down too!"

The End

```
E  X  T  R  A  O  R  D  I  N  A  R  Y
T  Y  H  R  L  P  X  S  V  C  V  F  V
Y  A  K  S  O  U  E  T  U  E  Y  U  C
H  Z  C  E  W  Z  J  R  F  Y  R  O  R
G  Q  M  Q  S  R  I  A  R  C  X  S  E
E  S  D  V  U  O  S  N  Y  A  Y  X  E
U  O  Q  D  U  E  E  G  M  K  Z  B  K
Q  K  E  S  O  R  L  E  R  H  T  I  E
I  T  A  A  L  N  O  I  T  C  I  F  B
N  H  S  A  L  F  U  C  N  Z  L  O  V
U  N  O  F  B  Q  C  H  E  E  K  Y  I
X  B  B  J  C  R  V  H  V  G  C  V  M
Y  H  O  T  B  U  B  P  V  Q  Z  N  F
```

BIZARRE
CHEEKY
CREEK
CURIOUS
EXTRAORDINARY
FICTION
FLASH
JACQUELINE
ODD
POEMS
QUIRKY
STRANGE
UNIQUE
VERSE

Printed in Poland
by Amazon Fulfillment
Poland Sp. z o.o., Wrocław